Only by Chance

IN CRIPPLE CREEK

BY DEBBY ARTHUR WARNER

DISCLAIMER

Dolly's Silver Lining Casino, Ms. Hattie's Bed & Breakfast, and all characters depicted in this story are a work of fiction and created strictly from the imagination of the author. Any similarities are purely coincidental.

ISBN: 978-1-7349415-2-4

Library of Congress Control Number: 2022903819

Second edition
Printed in the United States of America

Cover and text design by Laurie Goralka Design

For more information:
gjauthor@gmail.com
www.debbyarthurwarner.com

To Verl,

for always believing in me,

and encouraging me to believe in myself.

Preface

Historic Cripple Creek, Colorado—once known as THE WORLD'S GREATEST GOLD CAMP—is about forty miles southwest of Colorado Springs. The elevation of the old gold mining town is anywhere from 9,500 to over 10,000 feet above sea level...depending on where you're standing. I first visited Cripple Creek shortly after moving to Colorado from North Carolina in the late seventies. My first impression was one of feeling as though I was in the middle of an old western town on a movie set, except that everything was authentic. Captivated by its scenic views and small-town atmosphere, I've become a regular visitor.

During the eighties, my parents would come to Colorado in the fall from Florida and stay with me for two months. My father always wanted to go to Cripple Creek. He loved the quaint old mining town, and trips there took priority over other places on our list of activities to do. Gambling had not been introduced yet, but Dad could always find plenty to do—or not do. It was enough just being there. He enjoyed riding the old steam locomotive and listening to the narration on the rich history of the gold mining town. He truly felt that he had been transported back in time to the old West—quite the contrast from his modern-day surroundings in Florida.

In the early nineties, when I met and later married my husband, we traveled to Cripple Creek whenever we wanted to get away. We fell in love with the charm and intrigue of the different bed-and-breakfast lodgings we frequented. Two of our favorites then—as well as now—were the Hotel St. Nicholas and the Cripple Creek Hospitality House & RV Park. The Hotel St. Nicholas was built in 1898 and was originally Cripple Creek's first hospital. The Hospitality House was built in 1901 as the Teller County Hospital. The last time we stayed at the latter, the sign above our door said "Recovery Room."

The bed-and-breakfast that really inspired my using Cripple Creek for the setting of my story, and for Ms. Hattie's place, was an old two-story Victorian house that we happened upon one New Year's Eve. We had waited too late to make reservations and everything else was full. What a blessing that turned out to be. A most colorful person—I'll call her Fran, although that is not her name—owned the bed-and-breakfast and told the most fascinating stories while serving breakfast. She also liked to tell about the haunting experiences previous guests had encountered while staying at her establishment. We learned that many places in Cripple Creek have a reputation of being haunted—which, in my opinion, only adds to the charm of the town. We visited Fran's place several times before she eventually sold it. I'm sorry to say, it is no longer a bed-and-breakfast.

Cripple Creek may be known more today by some as a gambling town, but it still holds the history and ambiance of years gone by. Gold is still mined between Cripple Creek and Victor by companies that are committed to preserving historic structures while conducting modern-day operations.

The drive to Cripple Creek in late September is spectacular! The aspen trees are breathtaking in their golden, yellowish hues set against the bluest of blue skies, creating a picture-perfect moment.

About the Author

Debby Arthur Warner resides on the Western Slope of Colorado with her husband, Verl. She is a spiritual person whose priorities are family and friends. She has four children, two stepchildren, and six grandchildren. Being multifaceted, she has held licenses in cosmetology, real estate, insurance, and has had a successful career in sales management as well.

Her hobbies are painting with watercolors and oils, and collecting vintage costume jewelry—but her passion is writing. Over the years she has enjoyed writing poetry and short stories. *Only By Chance* is her first novel.

Acknowledgements

I have been blessed with special people in my life that care enough to be honest and keep me focused.

My deepest gratitude and appreciation go to my dear friend, Nona Backlund, for being by my side from the beginning—graciously being my second pair of eyes and tirelessly reading through dozens of rough drafts, providing valuable insight, and enthusiastically supporting me.

Many thanks and appreciation also go to: my writing buddies, Patricia Amadeo and Terry Pickens—or the Chicklets as we are better known—for their support, encouragement, honest critique, and constructive suggestions; Ann Leadbetter and all the wonderful women of WWF(a)C for always inspiring me; Meredith Nixon for her guidance; my daughter-in-law, Dina Hildebran, for posing for the cover and for putting up with my amateur photo shoots; retired homicide detective, Merlin Wilson—affectionately known as *Mister* Wilson; Dr. Jennifer Southard for patiently answering my questions; to my editor, Bonnie Beach, for her expertise; and a special thank you to my publisher, Carole London, for her patience and direction.

Also, thanks to my husband, our children, and grand-children, whose love, humor, and zest for life give me reason to breathe. And to *all* my family and friends, much gratitude for their loving support.

And a very special thanks to all the people of Cripple Creek.

Chapter One

Kelly felt numb. It was all too surreal. She knew she was at a funeral, but she still couldn't grasp that it was her best friend, Tara, who lay in the coffin. The officer's words burned in her mind: It was an accident, he had said. Her foot must have slipped. She fell off a cliff. She shouldn't have gotten so close to the edge, he said. His words played over and over in her head until she felt like screaming. She knew that trail was one of Tara's favorites, and even though she had some fear of heights, Tara loved hiking the Colorado National Monument.

Kelly stood by the graveside, oblivious to the sounds surrounding her, and kept her gaze on the hole in the ground. As she watched Tara's casket being lowered, she tried to imagine how her friend could have fallen. The officer thought it was an accident, but deep down, Kelly knew her friend wouldn't go to the edge and cause her own death.

She vaguely heard the last words that were spoken as the Elders compassionately ushered the mourners away. She lingered, but they soon encouraged her to leave too. As she walked away, she looked over her shoulder one last time. She paused and watched the remains of the freshly dug earth being shoveled gently over Tara's final resting place. It was at that moment she felt her friend's presence.

Two months later...

Once again, Kelly awoke feeling anxious and restless. It had been two months since the funeral, and for the past couple of weeks, she had wakened with a sense of uneasiness. And with each occurrence, she had grown more irritated. It was as if feeling restless, anxious, and uneasy had become routine. She was especially frustrated that morning when she realized the feelings were more intense.

She sat up and swung her legs over the side of the bed. She put her feet into the slippers that were positioned precisely where she knew her feet would land, then grabbed for the robe that lay at the foot of the bed. She knew by the time she reached the kitchen and poured her morning coffee—timed for completion as she approached—that her anxious feelings would have ceased.

Kelly was more practical than most people, and although intuitive, she knew there was usually an explanation for everything. There were times she liked being intuitive. She felt it gave her an edge as a reporter. But she also felt intuition was nothing more than a keen sense of awareness.

Dressed and ready for work, she returned to the kitchen for her second and final cup of coffee. She sat at the table and opened her planner to review appointments for the day, then realized she had nothing scheduled. She also realized she still felt restless and uneasy. More annoyed than concerned, she gathered her coat, briefcase, and purse and reached for the keys on the hook by the back door. As she opened it to leave, the phone rang.

"Oh, shoot!" she said aloud. Hating delays, but hating an unanswered phone more, she put her stuff down on the kitchen chair and picked up the phone on the counter by the coffeepot.

"Hello?" she answered in a tone that sounded rushed.

"Looking at my watch, I'd say you had one foot out the door. Kelly, don't tell me you were coming in this morning. I was hoping not to get an answer, but knowing you, I was afraid I would," said the familiar masculine voice.

"Good morning, Stan. I've decided not to go."

"Why, for heaven's sake?"

"I just can't! I haven't been anywhere in ten years. I wouldn't know where to go or what to do after I get there. I'd feel like a fish out of water."

"Kelly, listen to me!" pleaded her boss. "I've rearranged your schedule for the next ten days, not even the two weeks I insisted that you take. For God's sake, you haven't taken a real vacation in I don't know how long. Kelly, I know how much Tara's death impacted you, and understandably so, but you haven't been the same since. You can't continue to bury your feelings and emotions. They will catch up with you."

"I appreciate what you're saying, Stan, but really—I'm fine. I don't need to take any time off...I don't!" she said emphatically.

"Kelly, I'm not just your boss, I'm also your friend. I've known you for too many years, and I know how unkind the last few have been to you. I've watched as you buried yourself in work—not only taking on extra hours and working weekends, but forfeiting most vacations. It's time to start living again!

"You're not the indifferent, controlled person you'd like people to think you are. You've become addicted to work and it's time for an intervention. I'm *insisting*—not as your boss, but as your friend—that you take this time."

There was a long pause before Kelly replied. She hated to admit it, but she knew Stan was right. She knew she had used work as an escape, as a means of forcing that twenty-four-hour cycle to end—to drop into bed so exhausted that there was no time left to feel.

"Okay, okay," she said with resignation, "but where do I go?"

"I have a suggestion. Do you have a map?"

"Yes."

"Good. Get it out, open it, then close your eyes. Rub your finger over the map for a few seconds. When you open your eyes, look at where your finger has landed. That's where I suggest you go."

"What? Are you crazy? Do you expect me to just pick up and go without a plan, without reservations, without an itinerary...," but before she could finish, she thought she heard laughter on the other end.

"Come on, Kelly," Stan chuckled, "step out of your comfort zone. Don't be so predictable. For once in your life, take a risk and do something you've never done before. Think of it as an adventure. Pretend it's something you've always wanted to do but never did." He waited for a response.

Thoughts of going somewhere unprepared sent shivers through Kelly, and yet at the same time, she felt a sense of excitement!

"Are you still there?" he asked.

"Yes, I'm here. You know, Stan, as crazy as it sounds, you may be right. Maybe it is exactly what I need. It's strange, but for the last couple of weeks, I've been having some weird feelings..."

"What kind of feelings?" asked Stan before she could finish. He had witnessed Kelly's uncanny knack—on more than one occasion—to predict the outcome of a situation before others even knew of it. He was not comforted by the fact that she was having weird feelings. Once, he had walked into her office and told her his 9 a.m. appointment, Bob Nelson, was twenty minutes late, and without hesitating, she replied that he was stuck in traffic and wouldn't make his appointment that day. Stan asked how she knew: had Bob called on his cell to cancel? He remembered how puzzled she was, as if she was surprised by what she had just said. But then, nonchalantly, she said that Bob hadn't called but he wouldn't be in. She went to her file cabinet and busied herself as though the conversation had never taken place. Later that day, Bob called Stan and apologized for not keeping his appointment. He told him he had been stuck in traffic for two hours due to an accident. It had thrown his schedule behind, and even if Stan had the time later that day, Bob did not.

"I can't explain it." Kelly continued. "It's as though something has happened, or is going to happen, and I should know about it, but I don't. It's irritating. I can't figure it out. Now I sound crazy. If you repeat this, I'll deny it." She laughed in an attempt to minimize what she had just said. "I think I'm just feeling restless because I haven't been able to make a decision about taking this trip. I'm sure once I get in the car and go, I'll be fine."

"You're driving?"

"Of course I am. How else would I go?"

"I thought you'd be flying."

"Not a chance! If I don't even know where I'm going yet, I'm sure as heck not going to fly. I'd hate to depend on some rental car service once I got there. I'll feel more in control if I have my own vehicle. And besides, if I don't like where I am, I can take off and not have to worry about a return flight at a designated time."

"Okay, kiddo, but be careful."

"Hey, you're the one who told me to step out of my comfort zone."

"Yes, but that's before I knew you were driving. I'm being paged...got to go. Call me when you get to where you're going and let me know you've arrived safely. After that, forget I—and the newspaper—exist...at least for the next ten days. Good-bye, take care."

"Bye...and thanks, Stan." She hung up the phone and without thinking, went looking for a map.

Chapter Two

Kelly was backing out of the driveway when she remembered Tara's diary. She paused and wondered if she should go back and get it. She had laid it on the dresser while she finished packing, trying to decide whether to take it or not. She put the car in park and went into the house to retrieve it.

There it was, on the corner of the dresser where she had left it. She stared at it a moment, then grabbed it, drew it to her chest, and held onto it as though it would bring Tara back. She closed her eyes and thought about the funeral. She thought about the moment when Molly handed her the diary.

"Kelly, I want you to have this," she said as she handed her Tara's diary. "Her father and I can't bear to look at it. It's just too painful, and I'd feel like I was prying," said Molly as she fought back tears.

Kelly had been surprised by the gesture. She hesitated for what seemed like minutes, but it was only seconds. Then she spoke in a gentle whisper.

"But Molly, Tara's diary is so personal, and so much a part of who she was. Are you sure you won't regret not having it?"

"No," said Molly as she took Kelly's hand into hers and held it. "You knew Tara better than anyone. You are the one she would want to have it."

"Thank you," was all Kelly could muster, then embraced her friend's grieving mother.

When she returned from the funeral, she put the diary away. She, like Molly, was unable to look through it. But she'd take it with her now, and hope to find the courage.

She squeezed the diary one more time and then left the house. When she was settled behind the steering wheel, she placed the diary on the front seat next to her and wondered if there could possibly be anything in it that she didn't already know. After all, they told each other everything; there were no secrets between them.

Kelly had just put the earpiece to her cell phone in when it rang.

"Hello?"

"Hi, kiddo, just making sure you were on your way, and in the opposite direction of the *Daily Sentinel*."

"Yes, Stan, I'm finally on the road."

"So tell me, where have you decided to go?"

"Oh, wouldn't you like to know, Mr. Editor," she teased.

Stan was not your typical newspaper journalist. He genuinely took an interest in everything around him, but especially in the people that came in and out of his life—and not just from a reporter's perspective, but on a much deeper level. He also had a remarkable instinct for discerning fact from fiction; he was regarded as an exceptional editor by his peers. Stan had noticed a similar trait in Kelly when he first became her editor ten years ago and critiqued everything she did. She was only twenty-two at the time, but she soon became his protégé. Kelly was different from the other young, freshly graduated journalists who had worked with him at the newspaper. She had more than a passion for the news, more than an intuitive insight—she had a sixth sense that went beyond intuition. Stan recognized it, but Kelly chalked it up to her persistence at getting to the truth, at getting to what wasn't being told.

"Seriously, what direction are you headed?" asked Stan.

"I think I'll keep you guessing for awhile, but I will tell you this: I'm going to drive about 500 miles today. If I like where I am when I stop to spend the night, I'll stay a few days, then move on to a different location."

"I'm afraid I've created a monster," joked Stan. "You go from not going anywhere unless all the details are in place to totally winging it."

"Well, I'm not *totally* winging it. I do have 500 miles in place. What do you think about the new, unpredictable Kelly you've created?"

"I'd like her better if I knew where she was going."

"I bet you would," laughed Kelly. "What's the matter, Big Brother? Are you feeling a little out of your comfort zone? Does it feel strange to have one of your reporters take off without you knowing where they're going?"

Kelly's pet name for Stan was "Big Brother." Being her senior by fifteen years, she felt he treated her like an overly protective big brother. She'd get annoyed at times, but at other times, she found it endearing.

Stan and his wife, Rose, had been married for twenty years; they had sons but no daughters. Stan also had three brothers and no sisters. Kelly felt she represented a combination of what he didn't have, and since he viewed her as a younger version of himself, he treated her more as a family member than an employee.

"Maybe just a little," he responded to her question. "You're not going over any of the passes, are you?"

"Not that I am, but why do you ask?"

"Kelly, you might be a top-notch reporter, but as usual, you could care a rat's tail about the weather. It might interest you to know that there's a major snowstorm coming in later today over the southwestern mountains, and some of the mountain passes might be closed. If you're going that way, which I hope you're not, you'd better stick to the interstate. At least if the weather gets bad, you can pull off and stay in a motel. You won't have that option if you go the back roads."

"You see why I don't pay any attention to the weather? The last two southwestern storms predicted never materialized. Remember? The winds shifted, we had a few snow flurries, maybe an inch or two, and that was that," said Kelly.

"Put your radio on. This one's different. If you are headed through the back mountain roads," warned Stan, "you'd better change your course."

"You made your point...not that I'll need it. By the way, if I'm on the road and you're on the phone, how is any work getting done?"

"I see I hit a nerve. You just told me which direction you're going."

"Why do you say that?"

"Anytime you change subjects in the middle of a thought, it's because I'm getting too close."

"Don't flatter yourself. You're not always right. Go back to doing what you know best and let me hang up so I can pay attention to the road."

"Only if you promise to call me when you get there will I leave you alone to enjoy your vacation."

"Fair enough." She was about to hang up, then decided since she had Stan engaged in conversation, she would try once again to influence his thoughts about Tara's death. "Stan, on a more serious note, I can't shake the fact that I believe Tara's death was not accidental. She was not a careless person."

"Kelly, we've been through all this time and time again. There is nothing about her death to suggest otherwise. It was an accident. You have to accept that."

"No, I don't, and I won't. I know there is nothing to suggest otherwise. I accepted that in the beginning, but I can't fully accept it now. I think that's why I've been having these strange feelings. I know the police have no proof of foul play. I know it looked like an accident, but Stan, I *knew* Tara. I knew how cautious she was. I've hiked with her in that area, and she knew the terrain inside out. She would never have gone so close to the edge of a cliff to cause her to lose her footing." She stopped talking when she heard Stan mumbling to someone in the background.

"Sorry, Kelly. Bob Nelson is here and he only has a few minutes. He wants to go over the information we gave him on the Radcliff case before they air the story. I'll talk to you tonight." With that, he hung up.

As Kelly continued to drive, she thought about what Stan had said. She knew he was right—at least the part about Tara's death not looking suspicious. The police ruled it an accident. There was no evidence to the contrary. It was determined that she may have been frightened by a snake, or possibly slipped on some wet rocks. But Kelly knew Tara would never have been close enough to the edge for either of those situations to have occurred.

She was getting low on gas and began looking for a station. She had a little above a quarter of a tank, but she remembered, from what Tara had told her, that gas stations on the back roads could be few and far between. Tara had driven the same route on her many visits to Cripple Creek. The small gambling town had been one of her favorite places to visit, and yet Kelly had never been there. It wasn't so much the gambling that Tara liked, but the people she had come to know. Kelly thought about the residents of Cripple Creek. She wondered if they knew Tara was dead.

The route she had chosen to drive to Santa Fe would take her within twenty miles of Cripple Creek. She felt, for Tara's sake, she should stop in and visit with some of those who had come to know her. She wanted to tell them Tara wouldn't be back.

She hadn't made up her mind as to whether she'd visit Cripple Creek on her way to or from Santa Fe. Since she had gotten a late start that morning, she was leaning towards the latter, especially if Stan was right about the weather.

A few remaining weekend guests were checking out of the small gambling town, anxious to get home before the storm hit. Those who had a distance to go had decided to stay an extra day or two until the storm passed and the roads had been cleared. Many senior citizens liked to frequent the town of Cripple Creek, and for most, it didn't matter if they had to stay a little longer, especially if they had driven. The ones who were limited on cash, or just didn't want to drive, usually took the casino bus up from Colorado Springs for the day. Having heard the reports of the impending storm—and the weatherman encouraging everyone to stay home—the casinos knew the buses would not be up that day. They welcomed the lingering guests.

There were only two couples still left at Dolly's Silver Lining Casino who needed to check out and make it home in time for work the next day.

"I'll tell you, Martha, this doesn't look good," said the gentleman as he handed the lady behind the small checkout counter his credit card. "Have you looked outside recently?" he inquired.

"No, I've been too busy checking people out of here," she replied. "But from what everyone is saying, I gather it's going to start snowing at any moment. I've also heard this could be the biggest storm we've seen in decades."

"I don't mind driving home in snow, done it many times, but I have over 200 miles to go and I can only hope it doesn't get as nasty as they're predicting."

"Quit your griping and get on your way, Jack!" the robust man standing behind him hollered in jest. "I may not have as far to go as you, but I'd still like to get home," It was obvious the two men knew each other.

"Hey, Bill, I didn't see you there," said Jack as he turned around and shook his hand. "I thought you and Barb had already checked out."

"I've been trying, but can't get Barb away from her so-called 'lucky' Double Diamond machine." His fingers gestured in quotes as he mentioned lucky. "She hates leaving before checkout time—doesn't seem to be taking the weather seriously. Where's Karen?"

"At the video poker machine while I check out. Losing, as usual, but she'll give it hope until the last second. I've no room to talk. You took me out early at Texas holdem last night, and I didn't do any better on the machines. Sometimes you lose, and sometimes you *really* lose!" They laughed, shook hands, wished each other a safe trip home, and vowed to be back next month.

The town of Cripple Creek prepared for the worst.

Kelly finally spotted a gas station and pulled in. When she stepped out of the car, she noticed how ominous the sky looked.

Chapter Three

B eautiful, white morsels began to make their debut; ever so sparse at first, they seemed to multiply with every mile that Kelly drove. It reminded her of a huge reunion: as each one came, more were beckoned. Caught up in Mother Nature's display, she couldn't remember when, or if, she had ever noticed the many different shapes or sizes before. Each flake was truly an individual, and yet, when joined together, they blanketed the earth in harmony. *Why can't life be like that,* she wondered. *Why can't human beings, with all their diverse individuality, come together in harmony?*

The radio eventually turned to static and even the snow had lost its appeal. Kelly was captive. No work to be done and plenty to think about. And think she did.

It had been five years since she first noticed something different about her father. It was Christmas day, and she remembered it well. Kelly and her sister, Sara, always spent Christmas evening at their parents' house. It became a family tradition. Even after Kelly went off to college, she'd still always come home for Christmas. And when Sara married Todd, they would join her family for Christmas dinner. Later, after Josh and Rebecca were born, there were times when Christmas visits were divided between the two families. When Todd's parents came for the holidays, they would also spend Christmas evening with her parents, Ted and Jean. Kelly never missed a year. It was expected that, no matter what, she would be there. And there was no place she'd rather be on Christmas day.

They'd eat dinner between five and six, closer to five if all had arrived. It wasn't set in stone, but everyone knew dinner would be served no later than six o'clock, with or without their presence. Jean was adamant about that; she didn't want her sweet potato casserole getting cold. It might be preferred cold by some, but not by Jean. She felt it wasn't fit to eat unless it was hot.

While she was in the kitchen preparing dinner, Ted would get the fireplace cleaned out. Once it was to his satisfaction, he'd crumple up some newspaper and place it under the grate. Then he'd put some very dry kindling on top of the grate, followed by smaller logs of pine, pinion, and sometimes oak. He said the hardwood would never take off with just the paper and kindling. It needed the pine to really get it going. He had perfected the perfect fire. Once he put the match to it, he knew he wouldn't have to nurse it with more paper and kindling. Kelly had inherited her meticulous nature from her dad. His system was foolproof. The fire was always started right before dinner was served. You could hear the crackling and popping of the pine from the dining room, and by the time they transitioned to the family room for dessert, the room permeated with the warmth and fragrance of the hardwoods.

Kelly loved the smell of the wood burning. She'd sit so close to the fireplace that, days later, she could still smell the oak and pinion on her clothes.

After dessert, the gifts were opened. No one was in a hurry to end the evening. Jean would retreat to the kitchen and return with coffee and brandy for the adults and hot chocolate for Josh and Rebecca. Each would sip their drink and tell a fond memory of Christmas past. Even Josh, at age ten, and Rebecca, at eight, had built memories to share.

Christmas, five years ago, Kelly noticed something different. During dinner it occurred to her that the familiar sounds from the family room were not evident. She remembered how she couldn't imagine that her father would forget to light the fire. In all the years of the family tradition, Ted had never forgotten it. But he did that year, and Kelly had to remind him. No one thought much about it at the time. Ted excused himself from the table to go tend to it. Sara teased, saying Christmas would never be the same, tradition had been broken. A good laugh was had by all, except for Jean—which did not go unnoticed by Kelly.

Later that evening, there was something else that seemed unusual. She watched her dad struggle to come up with a Christmas memory, and when he did, it was one from when he was a little boy. She thought that was strange because, unlike the rest of the family, he always liked to reflect on something memorable from the year before—and like Kelly, Ted was predictable.

Later that week, when Kelly thought her father would be bowling, she dropped in on her mother. Knowing that the door would be unlocked, she walked in unannounced. She found both of her parents at the dining room table, looking through some pamphlets. The concerned looks on their faces when they saw her sent a wave of uneasiness through every part of her body and formed a knot in the pit of her stomach. She learned that her parents had just returned from the doctor's office. The events of Christmas day were not isolated. The first symptoms were noticed two years ago but weren't taken seriously. The past year they had gotten worse and could no longer be ignored. The doctor believed it to be an aggressive form of Alzheimer's.

For the next three years, she watched the disease take control. Even the doctors were surprised at how rapidly it progressed. It was obvious that Ted needed more care than what Jean alone could give, but she refused to put him in a nursing home. Kelly would spend the weekends helping with her dad, and Sara would go over in the evenings once Todd got home to stay with Josh and Rebecca. Jean still had the notes posted everywhere—telephone, refrigerator, toothbrush, shirt, pants—but it soon became obvious they had lost their meanings. The worst for Kelly was the day she walked in and Ted asked who she was. She had watched this strong and gentle, loving, compassionate man whom she adored change almost daily. Jean had pictures from his youth blown up and posted in every room. Music from the fifties and sixties was played on a regular basis, but it, too, was no longer recognized.

Kelly continued to drive and tried to put her memories to rest. She noticed that the snow was falling at a steady rate and that traffic had slowed. If this kept up, she knew it would be very late before she arrived in Santa Fe. She concentrated on the storm, but soon her thoughts went back to her father and that painful time in her life.

They all had tried so hard to keep everything familiar. But when Ted didn't recognize something, he became agitated. There were times he'd yell and throw things. He would put his clothes on inside out, maybe wear them an hour, then rip them off. They had to keep the door locked so he couldn't go outside and wander off. But when Ted could no longer recognize his own daughter, that was the day Kelly lost her dad. Six months later they buried him, but for her, the dad she knew had died a long time ago. She had already grieved her loss, at least that's what she thought. But when Christmas came that year, she experienced a deeper level of grief than she thought possible—it was never the same again.

Jean did not do well after Ted's death. The constant caregiving had worn her down. Six months after he passed, Jean suffered a massive stroke. The right side of her body went numb. Wheelchair-bound and in much need of medical assistance, Kelly knew she and Sara could not provide the necessary care their mother needed.

When Jean was admitted to the nursing home, she glared at Kelly as though she had been betrayed. She may not have been able to speak, but Kelly knew what that look meant. The doctors told her it had to be done; she was doing what was best for her mother. They reassured her that, one day, Jean would understand. But Jean never did understand. Three months later, she suffered another stroke. Kelly was by her side when she died. She knew her mother never forgave her. Her mother died blaming her for not taking care of her, for putting her in a nursing home, in a place where Jean never would have put her father. Kelly was left with the guilt, and the guilt hurt more than the loss, and the guilt wouldn't leave.

Chapter Four

The tears flowed freely. There was no one to hide them from; she was all alone. "Oh, Tara," she said out loud, "I miss you so much! I wish you were here." No sooner had she gotten the words out when calm came over her and she felt comforted. She felt warmth go through her shoulders, almost as though someone had put their arms around her. For a split second, she even thought she smelled a familiar fragrance.

The flashing lights ahead caught her attention and the moment was soon forgotten. As she strained to see what the problem was, she realized the weather had taken yet another turn for the worse. Soon, traffic was at a standstill. Slowly, each vehicle took its turn as it approached the black-and-white roadblock in the middle of the intersection. Kelly rolled her window down and the officer leaned in. He looked so cold; it was obvious he had been there awhile. His eyebrows had turned white and icicles had formed on his mustache. She turned the heater on high and hoped he could gain access to the wamth.

"Which way are you headed?" asked the officer.

"I'm going to Santa Fe. I live on the Western Slope and came through Breckenridge on Highway 9 to 24. I'm going through Woodland Park to Colorado Springs. I thought it would be shorter than going Interstate 70 to Denver and then down through Colorado Springs."

"You can't get through to Woodland Park for at least a couple of hours...could be much longer. A semi is jack-knifed, spilled half his load, and the road is closed. I can also tell you—you won't make it to Santa Fe tonight. I-25 is closed from Trinidad to at least twenty miles south of Raton Pass due to blizzard-like conditions. There are a couple of restaurants and several service stations here in Divide. You might as well choose one and hang out until the road opens—if it ever does. Since you don't live in Woodland Park or Colorado Springs, you might want to go into Cripple Creek and get a room for the night while you still can, seeing as you can't make it to Santa Fe anyway. In the last hour, this storm has gotten progressively worse, and it's not expected to let up until sometime tomorrow. If the road doesn't reopen, you won't even make it to Colorado Springs."

"How far is it to Cripple Creek?"

"Just take a right here and go about eighteen miles. As far as I know, it's still open all the way, but it's going to be very treacherous under these conditions, especially when you get to the switchbacks. I wouldn't take too much time to think about it; conditions are only going to get worse."

"Thank you, officer, I've taken enough of your time. I'll pull into the service station over there and get out of the way. Then I'll decide." She looked at her gauge. The marker registered just a hair above half a tank. Unless she had to sit idle and run the heater for long periods, she was satisfied with half a tank—it beat standing out in the elements.

She pulled in on the side of the service station away from the gas tanks. There were no visible parking spaces, so she created a makeshift spot for herself. She took a deep breath, turned off the ignition, and considered her choices.

Kelly had planned to visit Cripple Creek on her way home from her trip, after she'd had time to read Tara's diary. Tara talked a lot about Cripple Creek; it was one of her favorite places. Kelly was sure she would have written about it in her diary, and if she read the diary first, she would have a better sense of the town. She wanted to experience it through Tara's eyes.

She looked through her snow-covered window and decided she didn't want to stay where she was any longer. She started the car, put it in gear, and slowly headed in the direction of Cripple Creek.

Driving in snow was nothing new to Kelly. She had lived in Colorado most of her life. And since she had been with the newspaper, there were many times she'd travel as far southwest as Montrose and as far east as Eagle County to check out the credibility of a source. If she ever had to go to Denver, she would fly out of Grand Junction, but most of the time she drove—and that's the way she liked it. Kelly was used to bad weather, but she didn't relish driving on icy, snow-packed switchbacks.

But it beat the alternative, and she wasn't used to waiting around for something to happen. Her decision was made: she'd sit tight in Cripple Creek until the roads had been reopened.

She drove slowly and focused. *Not too bad,* she thought. *As long as I take it easy, I should be fine.* Fifteen minutes later she was climbing and the snow had intensified. The curves were sharp. Knowing there were drop-offs to her right, she hugged the center of the road. She'd been on many similar winding, twisting mountain roads, and she never could understand why they didn't have guardrails.

Visibility was almost nonexistent. The blowing snow seemed to be swirling in circles, as if it couldn't decide which direction to go. Wipers on high, Kelly strained to focus on the center of her lane, wishing she were closer to the car in front so she could be guided by its taillights. Only two miles left to go, but the wind was relentless. *Was it snowing harder or just blowing more?* she wondered. Either way, she knew conditions were worsening. Her cell rang, and even though she was going at a snail's pace, she was afraid if she answered she would lose all concentration. She couldn't remember when she had been that nervous behind the wheel. The phone rang again. *That's probably Stan,* she told herself, *and he can wait. I don't need to hear him taunt,* "I told you so!"

She gripped the wheel tighter and ignored the ringing phone.

Chapter Five

S he finally approached what she thought could be a small town, straining to gain perspective through each swipe of the wiper's blade, then gave a sigh of relief when she realized she had arrived. "Well, hello Cripple Creek!" she cheered aloud. "I sure hope you're not as cold on the inside as what you're showing me out here." But anything, she thought, was better than having to be on the road.

As she crept through the town—taking a mental inventory of each casino she passed—nothing sounded familiar. She distinctively remembered Tara mentioning the names of several of her favorite places, and yet, Kelly hadn't passed one that registered any sense of knowledge. The only one that came to mind was Ms. Hattie's Bed & Breakfast, but even it couldn't be found. Tara talked a lot about Ms. Hattie's place, mainly because that's where she usually stayed...and where Tara had met Kent.

Given weather conditions, Kelly was surprised at the number of vehicles parked curbside at each establishment, but she assumed others had also decided to wait out the storm. She pulled into the first opening she saw, which was not an easy task, due to the amount of unplowed snow in the way. When finally parked, she was sure she wasn't positioned correctly, but at that point she didn't care—she was just glad to be off the road. She took a few minutes to absorb the moment, taking in what little she could see, and then opened the door. Wind and snow thrashed at her face. She stepped from the car into a drift that appeared to be at least a foot deep. She braced herself and forged ahead until she came to the front door of what she thought read, "Dolly's Silver Lining Casino," and stepped inside. After wiping the snow from her eyes and taking in her surroundings, she was not very impressed with what she saw. It certainly wasn't of the Las Vegas caliber she had seen on TV and in the movies. She made her way down the narrow aisles of the small casino. There were machines stationed on either side, and the majority of patrons seemed to be situated on swivel stools in front of them. Some of the stools had backs and some did not. Age wise, most of the guests appeared to be upward of fifty, maybe even into their sixties and seventies. There were some middle-aged guests sprinkled here and there, and a few younger, but overall it was an older crowd.

She had also observed the names, as well as the sounds, of the machines as she went by: Double Diamond, Lucky Sevens, Haywire, Video Poker, Double Double Bonus Poker, Jokers Wild, Wheel of Fortune, and some she couldn't make out. It appeared as though anyone playing a machine was quite preoccupied and wouldn't appreciate being disturbed by idle chitchat...especially from a stranger.

Kelly continued to meander around the walkways until she came across a long counter that appeared to be a bar. Not understanding the intrigue of the machines—or how to play them, for that matter, since she'd never been in a casino before—she decided to sit at the bar and order a drink.

"What for ya, ma'am?" asked the bartender.

Kelly looked at her watch; it was 2:30 in the afternoon and she hadn't eaten since breakfast. *It's really too early for wine,* she thought, *especially on an empty stomach.* But after driving through a snowstorm, she was ready for a drink. "May I have a coffee with Baileys?" she finally asked after telling herself that Baileys was the better choice.

"You playing the machines?" he asked.

"Excuse me?" she replied.

"If you're playing the machine," he pointed down on the counter to the video poker display under the glass, "the drink's free, otherwise it's four dollars. Might as well put a five in and play; you'd only be risking a dollar, and I can't give it to you free unless you play."

"Why is that?" she asked as she looked down at the machine.

"We comp you if you play; otherwise you pay...simple as that. What'll it be?"

Kelly looked at the cards staring up at her through the glass counter and decided that she really didn't have much to lose, and she did know a little about cards; she and Tara used to play gin rummy a lot when they were teenagers.

"Okay, I'll play; here's my five."

"You don't give it to me, ma'am; you put it in the machine. Here, it goes like this." Taking the money, he leaned over the counter and inserted the five dollar bill into the slot. "Now, all you have to do is to hold the cards you want by pushing the hold button under the card, then you push the draw button. This is the twenty-five-cent machine, so every hand you play will cost you a quarter. You can play up to five quarters at a time if you want. The payout on each hand is listed up here." He pointed to the chart above the dealt hand.

"I guess it's obvious I've never played before."

"Yes ma'am. I'll go get your coffee."

"Wow, are you for real?" asked the stranger seated to the right of Kelly.

Kelly's first reaction was that of embarrassment when she realized the man had overheard her conversation with the bartender. But then she felt annoyed. *What business is it of his?* she thought. Rather than respond, she decided to ignore him.

When the bartender brought the coffee, Kelly noticed his name on the tag he wore. "Thank you, Ed," she said, and pushed a few buttons so he'd see she was playing. "Ed, have you heard when the snow is to let up?"

"It's just getting started. They're saying we can expect to have up to three feet by tomorrow afternoon. They're calling it the worst blizzard in fifty years."

Kelly stared at him in disbelief. "Please tell me you're kidding," she pleaded.

"Sorry, ma'am. I wish I was. Do you have a room for the night?"

"No," she replied, realizing she had never seriously entertained the idea. She figured she might have to stay a couple of hours, at least until they reopened the road to Colorado Springs, but she never banked on having to spend the night, and she certainly hadn't planned on three feet of snow. *Stan will never let me live this down,* she thought; then she remembered she'd left her phone in the car.

Ed interrupted her thoughts. "You can check at the desk, but I suspect we're booked for the night. Dolly's only has a few rooms, and I've noticed anyone lucky enough to make it here has headed straight for the desk."

"Where else could I stay?"

"There are several other places. The Double Eagle is the largest and would have the most rooms. You should have stopped on your way in. It's up the road a ways, but I doubt you can get your car out now. See that guy at the end of the bar?" Ed motioned to an unassuming gentleman at the end of the bar to Kelly's left.

"Yes."

"Well, he came in after you did, and he told me he just went to get a map out of his car and couldn't believe how snow-covered the car had already become."

Kelly thought about her phone again. "Ed, I'm going over to the desk and see if I can get a room; then I'm going to my car to get my phone. Hopefully this seat will still be vacant when I get back, but it doesn't really matter—I've lost most of my money anyway."

"Excuse me," said the gentleman to her right. "I know you're probably trying to avoid me, but I may have an idea."

"And what might that be?" Kelly asked, intentionally sounding annoyed.

"Lady, it's not as though I'm deliberately trying to eavesdrop," said the stranger in a sharp tone, "but I am sitting right next to you, and the distance between you and me is less than the distance between you and the bartender."

"So it is," Kelly conceded. "You made your point. Now what's your idea?"

"I stayed at a bed-and-breakfast when I was here last summer. I believe it's called 'Ms. Hattie's.' Anyway, since it's off the beaten path, she might have a room available."

"Did you say Ms. Hattie's?" she asked, feeling her heart start to pound.

"Yes," he answered, quite aware that he now had her full attention.

Ed had left during their conversation but returned just in time to hear Ms. Hattie's name mentioned. "Ms. Hattie's place is about five or six blocks behind the casino. You'd never be able to drive there...even if you could get your car out. There hasn't been much traffic on the side streets and the snow is pretty deep."

"How *can* I get there?"

"Not by walking, that's for sure," said the stranger. "Last I checked, you could hardly see three feet in front of you."

"Ms. Hattie's son has a snowmobile," said Ed. "He might be able to come up and take you back down on it. Do you want to check here for a room first, just in case there's something available?"

"No," she said as she turned to the stranger. "Sir, I thank you for the suggestion."

"You are quite welcome." He extended his hand. "Please, call me Joe."

"Okay, Joe, I'm Kelly." She finished the handshake and turned back towards Ed, but she could feel Joe's eyes on her. He was obviously appraising her. "Ed, do you have a phone number for Ms. Hattie's?" she asked.

"No, but the desk does. They have all the lodging numbers; it's a courtesy thing. If one doesn't have a room available, they'll help to make reservations for you at one of the other hotels. Hey, it's slow here. I'll go call for you. I know Ms. Hattie's son. I'll check and see if he has the snowmobile running. I'll also encourage him to take pity on you," he said with a wink.

"I really appreciate it; thanks so much," she said warmly, then again remembered her phone in the car. She decided to wait and make one trip; that way she could get her suitcase at the same time.

She looked down at the video poker machine. She had only seventy-five cents left of her credits, and her cup with coffee and Baileys was empty.

WELCOME TO
CRIPPLE CREEK
COLORADO

Chapter Six

Robert had been sitting in the room Hattie referred to as "the parlor" when she walked in. Without saying a word, she went straight to the window and stared out at the weather as though in a trance. He watched her for awhile before he spoke. He knew where her thoughts were.

"Hattie, he'll be back," he said, breaking the silence. "He's only gone to the store. And he's not driving a car," he added.

She didn't turn around. She hadn't noticed anyone in the room when she walked in, but she knew who it was. "Oh, Robert, you know me too well. Is it that obvious?"

"Only to me is it that obvious. Every time we have a bad storm—especially if Kent has gone out—I usually know where to find you."

"Why is that, Robert? Why do I still get nervous when the weather gets bad? It's been over twenty years since the accident; it's not as though I'm still grieving over Larry. I accepted my fate and have dealt with it very well. Wouldn't you agree, Robert?" she asked as she turned to face him.

He smiled. "Yes, Hattie, you certainly have." He remembered that night twenty years ago. The weather was similar, except that it was a spring blizzard with very wet snow. By nightfall the snow on the roads had turned to ice. Larry was on his way home from Victor after attending a council meeting to discuss safety issues in the mines. The car slid and went off an embankment. Larry never knew what hit him—he died instantly. And now, all Robert wanted to do was to put his arms around Hattie, to reassure her that Kent would be fine, but he knew he couldn't—she'd never accept it. She had always rejected any kind of affection he tried to show her, even if it came in the form of compassion.

Robert had moved into Larry and Hattie's boardinghouse just weeks before the accident. He was their very first boarder. After Kent went off to college, Hattie and Larry had talked about how empty their old two-story Victorian home felt. Kent was an only child, but he had plenty of friends. The house was always full with the energy of youth. With Kent gone, and no more friends to occupy the space, his absence was magnified. When Hattie read in the newspaper that there was a shortage of affordable housing for some of the miners, she had talked Larry into remodeling their home and turning it into a boardinghouse. It had two large rooms and a large storage room upstairs. He divided the two large rooms into four individual bedrooms and converted the storage room into a communal bathroom. Larry and Hattie's bedroom was downstairs, as well as Kent's and the spare guest room. Since Robert was the first boarder to move in, he was given the guest room downstairs. Another boarder, Al, had a room upstairs. There were three other boarders, but over time—especially after Cripple Creek became a gambling town—each left for one reason or another. Hattie had trouble renting the other rooms on a long-term basis, so she finally decided to rent them out nightly and for weekends to the visitors that came to Cripple Creek.

"Maybe that's Kent," said Hattie as the phone rang. She went to the kitchen to answer. "Hello?"

"Hi, Ms. Hattie, this is Ed over at Dolly's. Do you have a vacant room for tonight?"

"Yes, my two boarders are the only ones here. The three rental rooms are all available."

"Great! I have someone who needs a room, but with the weather like it is, she doesn't have a way to get there. Can Kent get the snowmobile going and come and get her?"

"Kent's not here right now. Actually, he's taken the snowmobile to the store to get some supplies before it closes. I thought this might be him calling to tell me he'd forgotten the list. He should be back soon. I'll let him warm up a bit, then I'll send him up there to get her. What's her name?" she asked, as she opened the registry that lay under the phone.

"Uh...Kelly...yes, I heard her say Kelly. I didn't get her last name."

"That's okay, I'll just write down Kelly."

"Thanks, Ms. Hattie. You can tell Kent—that other than the weather—there's no reason to hurry. I'm sure he'll have no problem on the snowmobile. I don't think Kelly will mind waiting as long as she knows she has a room. I'll tell her to go into the cafe and grab a bite to eat...seeing you only serve breakfast and not dinner to the visiting guests."

"That will be fine. But if she doesn't eat before she gets here, I can make an exception—considering the circumstances. She can join Robert and Al for dinner. I think I'll have enough, but if not, I'll serve smaller portions."

"Hopefully that won't be necessary. Thanks for your help. Good-bye."

Hattie hung up the phone and went back to the parlor. Robert was still there. his head buried in a book. He looked up when he heard her come in. "Everything okay, Hattie?" he asked.

"That was Ed from Dolly's. I really don't understand why he was calling instead of Martha. He's usually stuck behind the bar, not the desk. Maybe Martha got lucky and went home early. Dolly's must be full for the night. He was calling to see if we had a room available. I guess Kent will have to go back out. It's the only way she'll be able to get down here."

"And he will be fine, Hattie," Robert said. She nervously rubbed her hands together, and then sat down in a tall Victorian chair that was upholstered with a ruby-colored fabric. Robert sat in a similar chair on the other side of the small, old marble table that separated the two chairs.

"Logically, I realize that, Robert," she said, sounding a little annoyed, "but I can't help worrying. Kent is all I have. Larry was my husband, and tragically he is gone… and unfortunately, has been for twenty years. You don't know how happy I was when Kent decided to move back home after his divorce ten years ago. *He's* my life now!"

There was nothing for Robert to say. He felt that ever since Larry's death, Hattie's love for Kent had become obsessive, even smothering. She never approved of anyone Kent became interested in, making it very clear they weren't good enough for him.

Hattie saw the look in Robert's eyes and became irritated. "Go on, Robert, say what you're thinking."

"Okay, Hattie. I was wondering when you were going to let Kent go. He feels so responsible for you and everything around here that he can't get on with his own life—or pursue someone of interest, for that matter."

She glared at him. "You've never been just a boarder to me, Robert—you've always been my friend—but I'm telling you, don't cross the line. Don't think you know what's best for my son. Don't you think I want what's best for him? When the right person comes along, he will have my blessing," she said sternly, then got up and angrily left the room.

"The right person will never come along" mumbled Robert under his breath.

"You're all set, Kelly," said Ed as he walked around the bar. "Ms. Hattie has a room and she's holding it for you."

"That's great; thanks Ed. What about the snowmobile?"

"It's at the store right now, so it'll be awhile before it gets here. Since Ms. Hattie turned her boardinghouse into a bed-and-breakfast, the only meal she serves to the visiting guests is breakfast. You should probably get a bite to eat while you still can. The cafe is over there behind the desk," he said motioning in that direction with his head.

"Come on, Kelly, I'll buy you a sandwich. I'm starting to get a little hungry myself," said Joe.

"No, thanks," Kelly said sharply as she hopped off the bar stool. "I can buy my own sandwich, thank you."

"Listen, Miss Snooty, I'm not trying to jump your bones. It was just an offer for a sandwich and maybe some conversation to pass the time, since it's obvious we're going to be stuck here awhile. But you know what, I'm glad you said no. I think I'd prefer to eat alone." Joe purposely stepped in front of Kelly and headed for the cafe.

"Have you always had that chip?" asked Ed.

"What?" Kelly asked, turning to face him.

"That chip on your shoulder, has it always been there?"

Kelly's face became flushed. She didn't answer. She didn't understand why she had acted that way. It wasn't as though Joe had been crude or flirty. *My God,* she thought, *I'm a reporter, I talk to everyone. And I know how to handle myself. He was just trying to be nice to a stranded visitor. Besides, he's stayed at Ms. Hattie's.*

"Kelly, Joe's a straight shooter. He's been coming up here every few months for years. He may seem a little rough around the edges—to you, but he's okay."

"I'm sure he is, Ed. Maybe I was a little harsh. Chalk it up to frustration. I should be almost to Santa Fe by now."

"Accept it; you're going to be here for awhile, and carrying that chip around isn't going to help. People here are low key—they accept what is. Relax and make the most of it...you can't do anything about it anyway."

"You're right. I guess I'll have to work on my attitude. I'll be in the cafe. You'll let me know when my ride gets here, won't you?"

"Sure will. Now go eat!"

He was seated in a corner alone and had just received his sandwich when Kelly approached.

"Is this seat taken?" she asked.

"Does it look like it's taken?" he snapped.

"I deserve that," she said as she pulled the chair out and sat down. "Hey, listen—I'm really sorry. I could have said 'no' in a nicer way. I'm just angry for having to be in this situation—it has nothing to do with you."

"Apology accepted," he said without looking up. "Order something to eat if you want, but I'm not buying."

Kelly laughed. "I wouldn't have it any other way," she said and reached for the menu.

Chapter Seven

They had just finished their sandwiches when the waitress came by with the coffeepot. She seemed to appear whenever the subject of Ms. Hattie's came up. Kelly also observed that the table where she and Joe were seated appeared to be getting more attention than the other tables.

"How about I top off your coffee?" she said. She poured without giving them a chance to respond.

"Well...uh..." Kelly strained to read the name on her worn-out tag. "Carla, if you insist," replied Kelly. "But, before I can take another swallow, I need to visit the little girl's room." When she got up to leave, the waitress put the coffeepot down on the table and turned to watch her. Joe took notice.

"I think she'll find it," he said. "Women tend to have a sixth sense when it comes to those kinds of things."

She looked back at Joe and picked up the coffeepot. "I wonder why she's here by herself. You don't see many women her age come to Cripple Creek alone. They're either with a friend or with their husband."

"What makes you think she's here by herself and not with me?" he asked.

"Body language—it's obvious you two don't know each other very well," she said as she left.

She had a point, Joe thought, but he also figured she had overheard Kelly asking him about Ms. Hattie's place.

"I don't think I can drink any more coffee," Kelly said upon her return, "but it didn't seem as though I had much choice in the matter. She was determined to pour it anyway."

Joe agreed. "She *was* persistent, I'll give her that. Hey, sorry I couldn't be of any more help to you, but I've only stayed at Ms. Hattie's once, and then only because Dolly's was full. I'm not much of a bed-and-breakfast type of guy. By the way, if you've never been to Cripple Creek before, how did you know about Ms. Hattie's?"

Kelly was cautious; she didn't know this guy, and confiding wasn't something she did readily...except with Tara. "I had a friend who used to come to Cripple Creek and she mentioned having stayed at Ms. Hattie's. She seemed to enjoy the place. Now that I'm here, I'm curious, that's all."

Joe sensed the mood change but didn't pursue it.

"Your ride's here," yelled Ed from across the room. Relieved, Kelly put a ten dollar bill on the table and asked Joe to pay her tab. She followed Ed into the casino.

Joe watched her leave. He wondered if he'd ever see her again. He didn't understand why, but he hoped he would.

"Kelly, this is Kent, your snowmobile taxi driver," Ed said in jest.

Kent? thought Kelly. *Is this the Kent Tara talked about?* She tried to remember how Tara had described him: tall, sandy blond hair, well built, and very good looking. From what she could tell, it appeared he fit the description.

"Nice to meet you, Kent. I see the weather is still pretty bad." Kent had snow on his hat, and the arms of his coat were wet from where it had melted.

"Hi, Kelly," he said, as he pulled a wet glove off to shake her hand. "I can't remember when I've seen it snow this hard. We must be getting at least two inches an hour. I hope the casinos have cots and blankets—it doesn't look like anyone will be going anywhere tonight. I'm even having trouble maneuvering the snowmobile, so if you're ready, we'd better get going."

"I'm ready. I just need to get a few things out of my car. It's parked right out front. Do you have room for a suitcase?"

"How big is it?"

"I have two, but I can get by with the smaller one. I can also hold it on my lap if need be."

"That will work. I'll help you get your things. You'd better bundle up; it's bad out there...and it will be even worse on the snowmobile."

"I'm as bundled up as I'm going to get," she said, wishing she wouldn't have been so adverse to the encumbering paraphernalia that went along with winter. She looked down at her feet. She wasn't wearing boots, but she was glad she had at least decided the lace-up high tops went better with her stylish black jeans than her loafers.

She never wore hats or scarves and only gloves on rare occasions. She considered herself to be warm blooded and preferred cooler weather to heat.

Kent looked at Ed. "She's joking isn't she?" They both stared at Kelly as though she were naked in her mid-length leather coat. Given the weather, she realized how ridiculous she must have looked.

"Kelly," said Ed, "you can't get on the snowmobile without something protecting your face and ears. That wind will tear you apart. Don't you at least have a scarf?"

"No," she replied as she watched Kent put on a ski mask, then a fur-lined Russian-style cap over it.

"Wait here," said Ed. "I'll check the lost and found and see if I can find something you can borrow. People are always leaving things here."

"It looks like you weren't prepared for the weather," said Kent.

"It's not like I wasn't warned—I just didn't heed the advice." She thought about Stan and what he said about the storm. She was anxious to get her phone so she could call him.

"Here, this should help a little," said Ed, as he waved a dark-blue flannel scarf in front of her. "I didn't find any gloves, but at least your face and ears will be protected."

"Thanks, this will be fine. I'm not going that far. Ed, will my car be alright parked in front of the casino—at least until tomorrow?"

"Now, that's wishful thinking. Don't worry about your car—it will be fine."

"Okay then, Kent, I'm ready."

She stopped at the car to get her suitcase and her phone. Kent wiped the snow from both doors so Kelly could find the handles, then he took the suitcase from her while she retrieved her phone. When she reached for it, she saw the diary lying next to it. She made a split-second decision to take it with her.

Stan paced back and forth. Kelly wasn't answering her phone, and the inclement weather had him worried. He wondered if she was ahead of the storm or stranded somewhere without cell service. He was especially frustrated not knowing in which direction she went. He picked up the phone and tried again.

Chapter Eight

Robert and Al had finished dinner but were still seated in the dining room when they heard the snowmobile. Hattie was in the kitchen. Robert knew she was probably seated at the breakfast nook with her cup of coffee, waiting until Kent returned before eating. She and Kent usually ate in the kitchen, but on holidays, they would join Robert and Al in the dining room... which always pleased Robert.

The door opened and Kelly was literally pushed in by the force of the wind. Kent had to hold the knob tight in order to keep the door from smashing into the wall. Kelly looked up just as Hattie approached the parlor; Robert and Al were close behind. Kelly's teeth were chattering and her body trembling from the cold, but she smiled when she saw Ms. Hattie.

She walked straight towards her and put out her hand. "You must be Ms. Hattie. I'm Kelly. It is a pleasure to meet you."

"Oh, my dear," Ms. Hattie replied, taking her shaking hand. "You must be freezing. Come stand before the stove." They walked over to the old wood-burning stove in the corner of the parlor across from the entrance.

Kelly couldn't see the fire in the old stove—there wasn't a glass door—but she could smell it. She rubbed her hands together over the top of the stove. She closed her eyes for a moment and took a deep breath—old memories flooded back. She could tell there was pine and pinion burning inside that old stove.

"Kelly, let me have your wet coat and scarf. I'll hang them in the mudroom to dry," Kent said as he reached for the garments.

Robert watched as Kelly pulled the scarf from around her head and face. Up to this point, he and Al seemed to have been ignored. She handed the scarf to Kent and tried to shake out her wet, flattened hair. She was drenched, but Robert could see she was attractive. There was a striking resemblance to Kent's former wife, Mary. *Oh my*, he thought, *this could be a problem.* He looked at Hattie for any visible change of emotion on her face, but he didn't detect any. Had she not noticed Kelly's fair complexion—her beauty? And even though her hair was wet, he could tell it was auburn—and he bet her eyes were green.

Al walked past Robert and introduced himself. "Hello, Kelly, I'm Al Kinslow, one of Ms. Hattie's boarders." Kelly smiled and shook his hand. He wasn't a tall man—she met him eye to eye. His face was more round than oval, or maybe the lack of hair on his head made it look rounder. She thought he was probably in his fifties, and he looked stout in his flannel shirt and corduroy pants.

"Pardon me, I seem to have lost my manners," said Hattie. "Yes, Al has been here for the past ten years. And

Robert has been here the longest—twenty years to be exact," she said as Robert stepped up.

"Robert Allen—Kelly, nice to meet you." Robert seemed more polished than Al. He was wearing well-pressed brown slacks with a blue shirt. He was taller than Al, with a slender but strong-looking build for a man in his sixties. He also had an impressive head of charcoal hair. His facial features were average, but appealing.

"Nice to meet you, too," said Kelly.

Robert was standing next to Hattie. Kelly thought they made a handsome couple. She remembered Tara mentioning something about Ms. Hattie being in her early sixties, but that she looked much younger. Kelly also thought Ms. Hattie looked younger. She was wearing a navy pantsuit with a rose-colored blouse, and she looked even more attractive than what Tara had described. She was tall, and slender. Her hair was a champagne color, and curled softly towards her face. It was obvious where Kent had gotten his looks.

"Kelly, have you eaten?" asked Hattie.

"Yes, thank you. I had a sandwich in the cafe at Dolly's."

"Well, dear, I'm sure you've had a very long day. You're probably anxious to see your room. It's upstairs, and I'll be glad to take you to it."

"Thank you, Ms. Hattie. I would like to get settled, and I do need to return a phone call. I'm sure I can find it—there's no need for you to make an unnecessary trip upstairs. You probably have to make enough trips upstairs as it is."

"Well, then, here's your key, dear. It's upstairs on the right—room number 2."

Kent picked up Kelly's suitcase. "I can get that, Kent," she said. "It's really not heavy, and you've done so much already." She took the suitcase from him—in spite of his protest—and again mentioned how nice it was to have met everyone. She could see the staircase from where she stood and headed towards it.

"Kelly," Hattie said as Kelly approached the bottom step. "Breakfast is served at nine. There is a brochure in your room on the nightstand. But I thought I'd better mention breakfast in case you didn't look through it right away."

"That sounds wonderful! I'll be there."

The stairway was old, and each step creaked with its own unique sound. When she got to the top, the building was transformed. The hallway was carpeted, unlike the hardwood floor and throw rugs that were prevalent downstairs. It wasn't new carpet, but it was clean. The walls were papered and a chair rail separated two distinct styles. Above it was a floral motif with pink and red roses on a cream-colored background. Below was pink, red, and cream-striped wallpaper. It blended beautifully with the rose-colored carpet, which was a cross between the pink and red roses in the wallpaper.

As Kelly walked past the rooms, she found it interesting that the doors were left open, except for room 1. Room 3 was on the left across from room 1, and room 4 was on the left across from room 2. The numbers to the rooms were written on wooden plaques mounted above each door. She wondered why the door to room 1 was closed, then realized it had to be either Robert's or Al's—unless their rooms were downstairs and another guest had checked in. The fleeting thought left as she walked into room number 2. There was a window straight across from the entry, and the bed was to the left of the door. The light was already on... as if to say, welcome. The lights were not on in rooms 3 or 4. She walked in and closed the door. The room wasn't very large but adequate. She noticed a small wooden table across from the foot of the bed and laid her suitcase on it. Above the wooden table was an oval mirror. She stared into it and stroked her wet hair. *I guess it could be worse,* she thought. *At least I have a room for the night. And not just any room, but a room at Ms. Hattie's. I'm actually staying in the same bed-and-breakfast where Tara stayed.* She turned from the mirror and admired the bed. It was a four poster that looked like it might have had a canopy upon it at one time. The posts were painted a soft cream that had rich velvet-looking burgundy stripes running through it. The bedspread was burgundy with cream roses. Two shams matched the bedspread and were propped up against big, fluffy pillows. It looked so inviting. All she wanted to do was fall into it, but she knew she had to call Stan first. She sat on the side of the bed and opened her purse. She had put her phone and Tara's diary inside. Taking them both out, she laid the diary on the nightstand by the bed—then listened to her messages. There were three—all from Stan. She looked at her watch. It was fifteen minutes past eight. She called his cell phone.

"Kelly, where are you? Are you alright? Why didn't you call me back?"

"Yes, Stan, I'm fine. I'm sorry if I worried you, but this is the first chance I've had to call." She warned him not to say "I told you so" then proceeded to fill him in on the day's events.

Downstairs, Robert and Al were still in the parlor and just about finished with their nightly game of checkers. They were alone. Hattie and Kent had retired to their quarters after finishing a late dinner.

"What did you think about the girl?" asked Al.

"You mean Kelly? Really, Al, I don't think I'd classify her as a girl. Young woman or young lady would be more appropriate, don't you think?"

"Okay, Robert. What did you think about the young lady?"

"What is there to think? We weren't in her presence that long. What you really want to know is what do I think Hattie thought about Kelly. Isn't that true?" Robert enjoyed giving Al a hard time about most things, but Al knew that when it came to Hattie, Robert had a tendency to reserve comment.

"I guess that is what I want to know. Don't you think Hattie was being especially friendly this evening?"

"Hattie is always friendly when she first meets someone, Al, you know that."

"Most of the time that's true, but I've talked to you before about the change I've seen in her." Al continued. "Ever since Kent became interested in that gal who used to visit regularly, she seems different at times—moody. I don't pay attention too much around here—I like to mind my own business. But when voices get loud, you start to notice. I'm not well-read like you, Robert. I'm just an old miner who doesn't have a lot of interest outside of the mine. But even I can see when a pretty girl—or woman, as you prefer I call them—makes repeat visits, Hattie becomes less friendly."

"Have you forgotten, Al, I was a miner too?" retorted Robert. "Since my days in the mine, I've pursued my passion for good literature. It doesn't mean I'm knowledgeable in human behavior. You ask me about Hattie as though I have answers—I don't. She's a mother who worries about her son. She doesn't want someone taking advantage of him—that's all."

"He's a forty-year-old man!" Al said. "He doesn't need his mother protecting him. It's not normal the way she acts at times. I never told you this, Robert, but a few months ago, I overheard Kent and Hattie arguing about how rude she had been to a gal he had dated. I don't know who they were talking about—I didn't hear a name. It made me uncomfortable though, I can tell you that."

"You're overreacting, Al. Everyone has disagreements. You and I even disagree at times. Hattie may be a little stressed these days. Business has been slower this past year than previous ones, probably due to the economy and this harsh winter we're having. She was very friendly to Kelly this evening. She just needs a few more guests to cheer her up. Now, enough of this—let's finish our game so I can get to bed."

"Yes, she was friendly to Kelly," pursued Al. "Let's hope it stays that way."

Chapter Nine

The shower felt good. It had been a very long day. Kelly was tired but not necessarily sleepy. She climbed into bed and propped up the pillow behind her. She looked at Tara's diary and wondered—if *she* had written a diary, would she want *Tara* reading it? She felt intrusive. With mixed emotions, she picked up the diary and began to read.

Tara's first entry was twenty months prior to her death:

__Jan. 1st__ My New Year's resolution—a commitment to myself. I'm not sure how to start this. Not with, Dear Diary, that's for sure. I haven't kept a diary since I was a kid. Dear Diary sounds so juvenile. I think the main reason I'm doing this—aside from wanting to capture memories—is in hopes of learning more about me...Tara. Dear Self, maybe that's how I should start it—or Hello Alter Ego. Maybe Hi, Friend, and write as though I'm talking to Kelly—I like that! Okay, Hi Friend it shall be.

Well, Friend, I shouldn't have started this tonight. I'm too tired to continue. I guess I figured I needed to at least make an attempt on the first of January or else I would keep putting it off.

I doubt I'll continue on a daily basis after the first week, but I will set a goal for at least three times a week. But for now, I'll say good night.

__Jan. 2nd__ Hi, Friend—It's 7a.m. and I'm thinking about taking a hike on the Monument today. Temperature's supposed to be in the 40s—not bad for a winter day! I'm thinking of hiking a new trail this time. Maybe I'll find one I like and can add it to my list of favorites. Called Kelly to see if she wanted to come along, but as usual, she was busy.

Kelly, I had the best conversation with you New Year's Eve. When I hung up the phone, I couldn't believe we had talked for almost two hours! It was like old times—silly teenagers spilling our guts. It must have been the champagne. That was so much fun! Each of us opening a bottle of champagne and toasting the other as we talked. I don't know about you, but I finished my bottle. Did you notice I didn't even bring up Mark's name? But oh, how I wanted to. It is exactly five years today since your divorce. I bet you're thinking about that. Five years, Kelly—let it go. Not all men are like Mark.

Kelly set the diary on the nightstand. She had read enough for one night, and she didn't want to think about Mark. Instead, she thought about the girl talk she and Tara had that New Year's Eve. She was pleased it had meant so much to Tara. She was tired, but as she drifted off, she couldn't help but think about Mark anyway.

It was a painful subject. Kelly often wondered how she could have been so blind. They had been friends since grade school. By the time they reached high school, it became natural for them to go to movies together and even most school functions. Kelly had never really dated anyone else, and neither had Mark. They enjoyed each other's company. Both chose the same college, and by their senior year had become engaged. Kelly's first job out of college was with the newspaper. She wanted to establish herself as a credible reporter, and Mark agreed to wait two years before marrying. Kelly worked every spare moment she could.

Soon after they were married, Kelly noticed a difference in Mark. Even though he had always treated her more as a sister than a girlfriend, she expected that to change once they were married. She anticipated the relationship would progress on a much deeper level—it did not. If anything, he was less affectionate, but he was always very caring and thoughtful. She was comfortable with him and couldn't imagine life without him. They had tremendous respect for each other, and Mark seemed to adore her. Sometimes when she worked late, he would make dinner and have it waiting for her when she walked in the door. She felt there was nothing he wouldn't do for her, and yet, he didn't share the same desire for intimacy that she did. She worried at times he wasn't physically attracted to her. He tried to reassure her and said it was his problem—a low libido. Then he would take her in his arms and make love to her.

Kelly felt that overall their marriage was good. Mark was very supportive of her career and understood her need to work extra hours. He was also very willing to postpone starting a family until she felt secure in her position with the newspaper.

They had been married almost two years the day Kelly's world fell apart. She was on her way to an interview, and since she was ahead of schedule, she decided to stop by the house to take something out of the freezer for dinner. Mark's car was in the driveway. She was concerned; he had told her he'd be working a little late that evening. She was convinced he must have had a migraine and expected to see him on the sofa. Once every few months, Mark suffered from debilitating migraine headaches. He would close the drapes in the den and lay on the sofa. But he wasn't on the sofa, or in the kitchen. She went upstairs to look in the bedroom.

When she got to the top of the stairs, she heard voices and assumed Mark was on the phone. As she approached the open bedroom door, she froze. He wasn't alone! Standing to the side of the bed, his arms were wrapped tightly around someone, and they were sharing a very intimate embrace. Kelly couldn't tell who it was. She tried to speak, but nothing came out. Then they kissed—unaware that she stood frozen in the doorway. The purse she still had hanging from her shoulder fell to the floor, and her keys jingled out. Startled, Mark released his embrace, horrified to see Kelly standing there. When she saw who Mark was with, she felt ill. One hand went over her mouth, and the other grabbed her stomach. There he stood, with Sam by his side. Sam! Not only was Sam his closest friend, he was also the best man at their wedding!

Kelly grabbed her purse and keys and ran. Mark yelled after her, but she ignored him. She went to Tara's and didn't return home for two weeks.

She didn't want to go home. She didn't want to face the truth. She wanted to pretend it never happened. Mark tried to explain, but nothing made sense to Kelly. She could have accepted his sexual orientation if he hadn't married her, lied to her, made a fool out of her—and worst of all, made her feel undesirable. It didn't matter that he wanted to, or thought he could change. He humiliated her and used her to pretend he was someone he wasn't. He violated their marriage, in their own home—in the bedroom she shared with him. And she hated him for that.

After the divorce, Kelly vowed never to trust another man—at least not on a personal level. How could she? If she couldn't believe and trust someone she was close to—someone she had known since childhood—how could she ever trust again?

Chapter Ten

Having been in a deep sleep, Kelly wakened to a sound that seemed vaguely familiar. It took her a moment to realize where she was. Most of the time she was a light sleeper, and it didn't take much to disturb her. But, exhausted from the day before, she was groggy and strained to focus on the sound. She looked at the clock on the nightstand; it read 4:05 a.m. *That sound, what is it?* she wondered, and then remembered how the steps creaked when she came up them. *Who would be coming up the steps at this time of the morning? Or are they going down the staircase?* She wasn't sure. She sat up in bed and stared at the light illuminated under the door. She had noticed it when she went to bed and figured Ms. Hattie had left it on, making it easier for the guests to see their way to the bathroom.

It was quiet once again, but Kelly had an uneasy feeling—very similar to those uneasy feelings she was having before she left home. She continued to stare at the light under the door, then two shadows appeared. It looked like someone was standing there. The shadows looked like feet. She was sure either Robert or Al had room 1. But even if one of them used the bathroom down the hall, why had they paused at her doorway? And why did someone come up or down the stairs? Was it Ms. Hattie? Had she forgotten to put extra towels in the guest bath? Even so, why do it at four in the morning?

Okay, Kelly—don't overreact, she thought to herself. The shadows were still there, and she couldn't remember if she had locked the door. Quietly, she got out of bed, but then sneezed before she could silence herself. The shadows left as quickly as they had appeared. Kelly approached the unlocked door and secured it. For a split second she had wanted to open the door and look out, but she decided against it. The steps creaked again. Whoever was at the door must have gone down the staircase. Kelly was fully awake; there was no sleep left in her. She picked up the diary and continued where she had left off, pausing every so often to reflect on Tara's words.

It was six in the morning when Joe went down for coffee. He'd had a restless night. It had been almost five years since the death of a beautiful young real estate agent, Tiffany Buckley, from Colorado Springs. It was a senseless murder that had been made to look like an accident. Joe was suspicious right from the start. Tiffany was last seen alive in Cripple Creek.

"Good morning," said the waitress as Joe took a seat. The cafe had just opened, and he was the first customer of the day. He was surprised to see the same waitress who had worked the dinner shift the evening before.

"You're putting in long hours."

"They've got me working double time. The other waitress, Tonya, will help hold down the fort. She wasn't able to get home last night either. You'll be seeing a lot of us. I'm guessing it will be days before new blood can make it in."

"You're probably right. I haven't checked outside yet; I needed my morning coffee first. What's it doing out there?"

"It's still snowing. Depending on what window you look out, I'd say the drifts are about five to seven feet high. They said we could get three feet of snow by the time this storm ends, but I believe we've already gotten that much."

"Hey, Carla, I need you in the kitchen!" yelled a voice from behind the swinging doors.

"They're also short staffed in the kitchen. Anything other than coffee this morning...?"

"No hurry, but when you get a chance, I'll have some toast. And keep the coffee coming." He had plenty of time to waste. He also knew he wouldn't have anything new to add to Tiffany Buckley's file. Due to the weather, it was another wasted trip. He wondered how many wasted trips he had made. The link from Tiffany's death to Cripple Creek was small at best, but he couldn't let it go. He felt a stronger connection in his gut, and he was determined to prove it.

"Here's your coffee. Toast will be right up." Carla stared at the folder in front of Joe. "Strange."

"What's that?" he asked.

"I don't know too many people who bring work with them to Cripple Creek."

Joe was glad he didn't have Tiffany Buckley written on the folder. He had purposely removed it. If someone in Cripple Creek knew something about Tiffany's death, he didn't want to draw attention to himself—at least, not yet.

"On what assumption are you basing your opinion?" Joe inquired.

"What else would be in a folder that size?"

"I can think of many things, but this happens to be my hobby. I collect trivia, jokes, anecdotes, tidbits, and human interest stories. I talk to people when I'm playing the machines. You'd be surprised how interesting that can be." It sounded good to him, and he hoped she'd buy it.

She gave him a "yeah, sure" kind of look, then said she'd be back with his toast and more coffee.

Joe was irritated but more intrigued. Why had Carla, a waitress, taken such an interest in him—and in Kelly last night for that matter? Was she that nosey or just passing the time of day?

Carla returned with the toast and more coffee. "Okay, say it *is* your hobby. Why don't you read me a joke? I could use a good laugh right now. I'll make you a deal: every time I come back with fresh coffee, you have to read me a joke."

"Nope, doesn't work that way. I am the customer, you are the waitress. It is not my job to pay you with a reading in exchange for more coffee." He was feeling annoyed and it showed.

"Well, aren't we in a bad mood...must be the weather," she said, and left abruptly.

That woman is getting under my skin. He watched her. The cafe wasn't busy yet, and she had time to linger with the other customers, but she didn't. She only seemed interested in Joe. Why?

Kelly wakened with the diary resting on her chest. She didn't remember dozing off. She closed the diary and thought about what she had read.

Tara talked a lot about hiking. It was her passion. And yet, she seemed to be searching for something more. She had never been married and dated all the wrong men. She repeatedly stated in her diary that she felt she was finally going to meet Mr. Right. She also mentioned how much she missed the weekly girls' night out with Kelly. They had dispensed with the ritual when Kelly became consumed with her parents' illnesses. They would talk on the phone, but never in depth like they did in person.

In a strange way, Kelly felt closer to Tara now than she had in a couple of years. She liked having the closeness back, and she was glad she brought the diary.

She glanced at the clock. It was already 8:30. Breakfast would be served in thirty minutes. She didn't have time to think about the night before, and the shadows at the door. She jumped out of bed and got ready to go downstairs.

Chapter Eleven

Back in his room, Joe threw Tiffany Buckley's folder on the bed. He flopped in the chair next to the bed and scratched his head. He had been over it a hundred times. He knew there had to be something in there that connected Cripple Creek to Tiffany's death, but he couldn't find it.

Tiffany didn't die in Cripple Creek. Her body was found in Colorado Springs, but she was last seen alive here.

Joe picked up the folder. *Okay—Tiffany called the office on Friday to get the combination to a lock box for a showing she had on Sunday. The property where she had the appointment was in a rural area in an upscale newer development. All the homes in the subdivision were valued over a million dollars and each was situated on either a two- or five-acre parcel of land. The home she was to show that Sunday was on five acres. She went to Cripple Creek for the weekend and returned early Sunday in time for her afternoon appointment. Her body was found Monday on the property of the home she was showing.* He opened the folder and reviewed his notes about the showing.

Sunday...Tiffany shows an expensive home to a Mr. Jason Goldbloom.

Monday...Didn't show up for her Monday morning staff meeting, didn't answer her cell phone. George, a colleague and friend, checks the log book, goes to the property, and finds Tiffany's body on a concrete patio below the second-floor balcony. Her skull was crushed.

Tiffany's log book revealed she had prequalified Jason Goldbloom. He was a well-to-do businessman from St. Louis, Missouri, who designed golf courses. Joe had him checked out. At the time of Tiffany's death, he was in the hospital with a ruptured appendix. He had been to Colorado Springs the year before to design a new golf course. He went up to Cripple Creek with an associate for the weekend before flying back to St. Louis. He stayed at Dolly's Silver Lining Casino. That was his only connection to Cripple Creek. Joe found no link between Jason Goldbloom and Tiffany Buckley, but someone used his name to set up the appointment with Tiffany. It was obvious they wanted her dead. She didn't fall off the balcony as first suspected. She was either pushed or thrown off and hit the concrete patio headfirst. Whoever did it had hoped it would look like an accident.

After the cops had arrived, they called in the team of detectives. Joe was the case leader. It took him only a moment to realize he knew the victim. She was the daughter of Tim and Jan Spencer—his neighbors from down the street. He'd met Tiffany at a Christmas party in her parents' home several years before. She had just moved back to Colorado Springs after a nasty divorce.

Her husband had been unfaithful on more than one occasion. And even though she had proof of his infidelities, Tiffany received nothing in the divorce settlement: since the marriage lasted less than a year, the judge ruled she wasn't entitled. She decided to stay with her parents until she could find a place of her own. Tim and Jan were always entertaining, and Joe was a frequent visitor. He ran into Tiffany many times at their home.

Joe broke the news to Tim and Jan. It was difficult and painful. He also did something else: he promised he wouldn't rest until the person responsible for taking Tiffany from them was brought to justice. But eventually the leads ran cold. Joe was obsessed with Tiffany's case and refused to put it in the cold file—even when Captain York gave him an ultimatum. He decided it was time to move on. He resigned from the police department and opened his own private investigative agency. Since then, he had focused on finding the murderer of Tiffany Buckley.

Chapter Twelve

When Kelly walked into the dining room, she noticed Robert and Al were already eating.

"I'm sorry," she said. "I didn't realize I was so late."

"Only by seven minutes," observed Robert, "but when Hattie says 9 a.m., she means it. Don't fret; you made it under the wire. Three more minutes and you would have missed breakfast. She'll keep it warm until ten past the hour, and then it gets thrown out. Have a seat, Kelly. Hattie will be back in a minute. I hope you slept well."

Kelly pulled the chair out next to Al and sat across from Robert. She expected a chuckle, or a smile, to indicate he was joking about breakfast. But she received neither. Instead, Robert just stared at her.

"Good morning, Kelly," said Al.

"Good morning to both of you. And yes, Robert, I slept like a log!" she said cheerfully. She didn't want to give any indication that she knew someone had been standing outside her door at four in the morning.

"I thought I heard your voice. Here's your breakfast, dear," Hattie said as she placed the plate of eggs, ham, and fruit in front of Kelly.

"Thank you, Ms. Hattie. I apologize for being late—I guess I overslept." Kelly couldn't imagine Ms. Hattie throwing out her breakfast as Robert had mentioned. She didn't seem the least bit annoyed that she was tardy. And she even made sure Kelly had everything she needed before returning to the kitchen. "I looked out the bedroom window before I came down. Do you know it's still snowing?" Kelly asked the men.

"Yes, indeed it is," Robert acknowledged. "However, I understand from the morning news that it's to begin tapering off by noon. I do hope, Kelly, it wasn't urgent that you be somewhere within the next few days."

"No, not really. I had planned to vacation in Santa Fe, but as you can see, my plans have changed."

"I hope you're a gambler," said Al. "There isn't much of anything else to do in Cripple Creek—especially in the winter."

"She could always go snowmobiling...now that she's experienced," joked Kent as he entered the dining room.

"I'll forego the snowmobile," laughed Kelly. "From what I've observed, I think Ms. Hattie's place will be great for some much needed R&R. I did bring a couple of books with me. I'm sure I'll enjoy the solitude." *I'll just* have *to enjoy it,* she thought to herself.

"Kelly, I checked, and your scarf and coat are dry. I'd be glad to take them up to your room if you'd like," Kent offered.

Hattie came back into the room to remove the empty plates and responded before Kelly had a chance. "That won't be necessary, Kent. I'm on my way up there to clean the bathroom and straighten Kelly's room—I'll take her things with me."

"Mother, you haven't cleared the dining room yet. There's no rush to get upstairs—we only have one guest."

"Actually, *I* can take my things to the room. I'm headed there now. Thank you, Ms. Hattie, for a delicious breakfast." Kelly sensed a little tension in the air and thought it was a good time to leave.

"I'm glad you enjoyed breakfast, dear. I'll knock on your door when I'm ready to straighten your room." Hattie's tone was neutral as she left for the kitchen with an armful of dirty dishes. When she returned to the dining room to freshen the table, Robert was the only one left.

"You surprise me, Hattie," he began. "I would have expected some kind of a reaction from you."

"Whatever are you talking about, Robert?"

"Oh, I think you know *exactly* what I'm talking about. I didn't know Kent's wife that well, but when I first met Kelly, I thought she favored her a lot. This morning I was surprised by how much. With her hair dried and styled, she could pass for her sister. I am impressed, however, with your willpower. You've shown no reaction to Kelly, and considering how much you despised Mary, I find it remarkable."

Hattie sat down. "Why do I try to fool you? You know me better than I know myself—at least on some subjects. It *is* uncanny, isn't it, the way she resembles Mary?"

"Yes, it is. But that doesn't mean she's like Mary... please keep that in mind. Actually, I think Kelly is a delightful young lady."

"You thought the same thing of Mary in the beginning. Remember?"

"Mary *was* delightful in the beginning," Robert emphasized. "She didn't change until after she lost the baby. Then, and only then, did her drinking get out of control. Having tried so long to conceive a child—only to lose it—and then to be told you will never be able to conceive a child again...she's to be pitied."

"I'm afraid I don't share your sentiments. It was Kent's child, too. He also suffered. Mary made his life a living hell! She'd drink all day, and he'd come home to a vicious, foulmouthed drunk! She'd verbally attack him all night, telling him he was worthless and accusing him of causing her to go into labor early. Even the doctors tried to tell her it was nature's way of clearing out a mistake. They said the baby would have been grossly deformed, but she wouldn't accept it. She wanted to blame Kent instead. Pitied? I don't think so. I'll never forgive her for what she put Kent through...never!"

"I'm concerned, Hattie. You seem to see Mary in every woman who might be a contender for Kent's affection. Kelly looks a lot like Mary, but she isn't Mary, and she doesn't seem to have any interest in Kent. Besides, she won't be here long."

"I know. And if you've noticed, Robert, I am trying to be pleasant. But there is one thing that puzzles me."

"What is that?"

"Well, when she arrived, she seemed unusually pleased to meet me. What was that about?"

"I wouldn't give it much attention. Since Dolly's didn't have a room, Ed probably gave you, and the bed-and-breakfast, a good recommendation. And it wouldn't have been out of the ordinary for Kent to have given his praise of you and the establishment. Or she was simply being polite. Why must you always assume there is more to everything than meets the eye?"

Hattie thought about Robert's comments before answering. "And why must you always assume I'm over-reacting?" She shook her head and sighed in resignation. "Oh, I don't know, Robert, maybe you're right. But I got the distinct feeling she already knew me—or knew *of* me—before she came to Cripple Creek. Where did she say she was from?"

"I don't believe she mentioned where she was from. At least I don't recall her mentioning it."

Hattie got up from the table and went into the parlor. Robert followed. For the third time that morning, she looked out the window. *Is it ever going to stop snowing? And when will they be able to clear the roads? When will Kelly be able to leave?*

Chapter Thirteen

Kelly was deep into Tara's diary when she was interrupted by the knock on the door. Without thinking, she slid the diary under the pillow, and then went to the door.

"I'm ready to freshen up your room, Kelly. There's some tea and biscotti in the parlor. You're welcome to wait there and enjoy the refreshments, if you'd like. I saw Robert and Al headed that way, but if you hurry, you might get there before they have time to devour it all."

Kelly had planned to talk to Ms. Hattie when she came to the room. She wanted to tell her about Tara. She wondered if she had heard about the accident. But when she saw her standing there, she felt uneasy, and something told her it wasn't the right time.

"Thank you, but I've already made the bed. It gave me something to do and I haven't been here long enough to make a mess...at least in the bedroom. The bathroom may be a different story. My hair tends to shed when I'm brushing it." She remembered the towel and washcloth she'd hung on the hook behind the door. "I did bring my dirty towel and washcloth back to the room. I wasn't sure how many use the hall bath, and I didn't want to leave them there. I can use them again. I like being environ-mentally friendly."

"That is very thoughtful of you. Mostly, only the guests use the hall bath. However, Al does use the shower. His bedroom had a larger closet due to the angle of the house. Kent took half of the closet and converted it into a half-bath. It gives Al a little more privacy—especially when we're busy. There wasn't enough room for a shower, just a sink and commode."

Hattie looked past Kelly and saw the bed had indeed been made. The room looked clean, and even the carpet showed no signs of needing to be vacuumed. "You're making my job too easy. I'll go and let you be, but please know that you are welcome to the refreshments—even if I can't give you a reason to leave your room."

Kelly smiled. "I'll be down in a few minutes. As lovely as this room is, I would enjoy sitting in the parlor for awhile."

Hattie lingered, almost as if there was something else she wanted to say, but then turned and left. Kelly closed the door and waited to hear if the steps sounded the same when she went down as they did the night before. She couldn't tell, and she reminded herself that unless it was a very large person, she probably wouldn't be able to distinguish the difference.

Before going to the parlor, Kelly read a few more entries from the diary. She was at the point when Tara had first visited Cripple Creek.

___**Feb. 21st,**___ *Hi, Friend—I've decided to try my luck at gambling. Shelly, a coworker, invited me up for the weekend. Two single gals in "Sin City," now that's hysterical! Las Vegas, Cripple Creek is not! It's a quaint, little town and used to be a very active mining town in its day...gold, mainly. There's a lot of mining still going on between here and the neighboring town of Victor, but it has been taken over by a larger corporate company. Shelly said when she first started coming to Cripple Creek, there were several assayer offices. At that time, you could even pan for gold and have it appraised. But now, since most of the smaller mines have closed, so have the assayer offices. Gaming seems to be the big attraction these days. I must say, I really enjoyed playing the machines today. There was a cozy, friendlier atmosphere in the casinos than what I've experienced in Vegas. Everyone should visit Las Vegas at least once in their life. I'm glad I did, but that one time was enough for me.*

It is after midnight and I've really had a full day. Shelly may be twenty years older than I, but boy does she have the energy! We didn't even book a room until we ended up here. Here...where is here? I think this is Dolly's Silver Lining Casino, but I wouldn't bet on it. Shelly is a free spirit and flies by the seat of her pants. She wasn't concerned about not having a reservation, but then again, it is February. She's a lot of fun, but not like you and me, Kelly. We would have had a room booked by January. Maybe some of Shelly will rub off on me and I can pass it on to you...ha ha!

Dolly's Silver Lining Casino—yes, I do believe that is what this place is called. I bet Shelly is still downstairs at the Double Diamond machine. Oh well, I wish her luck, but for me, it's lights out...

Kelly decided she'd better go downstairs for awhile. She opened her suitcase and placed the diary under her nightgown. She didn't know why she felt the need to hide it, but she did. *So Tara stayed at Dolly's the first time she visited Cripple Creek. She probably told me at the time, but I just don't remember her staying there. I do recall her mentioning how much fun she and Shelly had, and she wanted me to go with her sometime. She said maybe I would have beginner's luck like she did.*

In the parlor, Robert was seated in the ruby chair by the marble table. A book lay on his lap. Al was standing by the stove. Kelly thought she had heard voices when she came down the stairs, but all was quiet when she appeared. Robert opened the book and gave the impression he had been reading. She knew he wasn't. She wondered if they had been talking about her.

"Have you looked outside recently, Kelly?" Al asked, breaking the silence.

"No, I haven't," she said as she walked towards the window. "Well, would you look at this—it's stopped snowing. Oh, my," she continued, as she realized the scope of what she was looking at. "Look at all that snow! Snow, snow, and more snow...it is absolutely beautiful!" She didn't believe she had ever seen a more wondrous winter scene. The sun gently sprinkled its rays on the mountains of white as it peeked out around the few remaining clouds.

Robert put his book down and observed Kelly's excitement. At that moment, she had a child-like innocence. He imagined her running out the door to make snow angels, only to be consumed by the depth of the dry, soft mound. *Oh, Kelly,* he thought, *I do hope your visit is short-lived.*

Chapter Fourteen

Kelly was still in the moment when Hattie walked in and announced she had a phone call.

"Who would be calling me here?" she inquired.

"I didn't ask who it was and they didn't say. It's a man's voice, but that's all I know. The phone is in the kitchen on the counter. Follow me and I'll take you to it."

Kelly hesitated, not wanting to leave the magnificent view out the window, but—reluctantly—she followed Hattie into the kitchen. When she picked up the phone, Hattie left, but she didn't go far. She sat at the end of the table in the dining room by the wall that separated it from the kitchen. She muttered to herself, "Who would be calling her here? Who knows that she's staying here?"

"Hello, this is Kelly."

"Is this the crazed gal that doesn't know how to gamble?"

"What? Who is this?"

"This is the cranky middle-aged man who refused to pay for your dinner."

"Joe?"

"I see I described myself accurately," he said with a chuckle. "Hope you don't mind my calling."

"No, not at all. But to what do I owe the honor?"

"Boredom!"

"I don't know whether to laugh or be insulted."

"Maybe a little of both. We can discuss it over the cup of coffee I owe you."

"What cup of coffee?"

"You left a ten on the table last night. Your tab came to $7.25. Even if we split the tip, the most you would have owed was $8.50. I might be a cheap date, but I don't keep money that isn't mine. Now if you prefer, I can give you the $1.50, but you'd be doing me a favor if you'd accept the cup of coffee—it's that much time I'm not losing money at the machines."

"Since you put it that way, how can I refuse? But have you looked outside? I think it will be days before I can get out of here. I may not be able to save you from your losses. There's even a snowdrift blocking the front door!"

"Kelly, you're probably right, but I doubt I'll get out of here before you're able to come back for your car. I'm not too anxious to leave until I know all the roads I'll be traveling on have been cleared. Besides, I can't leave town until I pay you back, so please look me up when you get here."

"You're being ridiculous, but I promise to find you when I get there. I'd better go now and get off Ms. Hattie's phone. Thanks for the call. Good-bye." She hung up the phone and was a little puzzled by the call.

What was that all about? I'm sure it had nothing to do with the $1.50. Oh well, it gives me an excuse to quiz him some more about Ms. Hattie.

She didn't look in the dining room when she passed it on her way to the parlor. She had no idea that Hattie had eavesdropped on her call with Joe.

Robert and Al were no longer in the parlor. Kent was there and seemed to be deep in thought. He was seated on the paisley rose and ruby sofa. In front of him was the teapot and biscotti. They were placed center of the oval marble-topped coffee table. Kent had a half-eaten biscotti in his right hand, and he seemed unaware of its existence. His head was turned right, towards the window. He didn't even notice when Kelly came in.

She walked over to the wood-burning stove and stood in silence. She studied Kent, trying to remember why Tara had decided not to see him anymore. Or was it the other way around? She couldn't remember, and at that moment she wished that she and Tara had continued their girls' night out. *I wonder what he's thinking about. Could he possibly be thinking about Tara? Does he even know about her accident...about her death...about her murder? Yes, murder. There, I've said it! Does Kent, does anyone know that Tara has been murdered?*

A cold chill went through Kelly's entire body, and she visibly shivered. She went from suspecting Tara's death was not an accident to realizing that she actually believed Tara had, indeed, been murdered. But how was she going to prove it, and why would anyone want to harm her? Could it have been a random act of violence?

Or was it possible that Tara could have had an enemy? The way her body was positioned when found, it looked like she had slipped and fallen off the cliff. There wasn't any sign of a struggle or foul play. The police didn't find anyone that had been hiking in the area when Tara was there, so there were no witnesses that they knew of. Only two people for sure knew what happened that day. And one of them was dead.

Kelly was no longer consciously focused on Kent; she was concentrating on who could have wanted Tara dead. She was also unaware that Hattie had been watching her with wonder—if only for a moment—then she went over and joined Kent.

"Kent, you certainly seem to be in deep thought," she said, bringing him out of his trancelike state. "Where are your manners? I do hope you offered Kelly a cup of tea." She spoke as though she had just walked in and noticed Kelly.

"Excuse me, Kelly," said Kent. "I didn't hear you come in. I hope you haven't been standing there for very long."

"No, I haven't."

"May I get you a cup of tea? I won't promise it will be any good, unless you like your hot tea cooled off. It's been here for awhile. I can vouch for the biscotti, though," he said, raising the half-eaten one he held in his hand.

"Thank you. I will try the tea, and one of these," she said as she reached for a biscotti. Kent poured the tea, and when she got settled in one of the high-back chairs, handed it to her.

"So tell me, Kelly," ventured Hattie, "what brings you to Cripple Creek?"

"Actually, I was on my way to Santa Fe. But because of the storm, and the road closure, an officer suggested I make a detour into Cripple Creek."

"Have you ever been to Cripple Creek before?" asked Hattie.

"No, but I had a friend who used to visit quite often." She didn't know why she was playing it coy, but she decided to continue and see what kind of reaction she'd get when she mentioned Tara. "You may remember her. I believe she mentioned having stayed here a time or two."

"Really, and what was her name, dear?" Hattie asked, just as she began to take a swallow of tea. Kent suddenly gave Kelly his full attention.

"Tara. Tara Medcalf."

"Tara!" Kent said with interest, and he smiled. It was obvious that he wanted to hear more. Hattie began to choke a little on her swallow of tea. "Mother, are you alright?"

"Yes, yes. It must have gone down the wrong way. There," she said, and stopped coughing. "I'm fine now. Tara Medcalf...of course we remember Tara. She used to visit here quite often, didn't she, Kent?"

"Kelly, how *is* Tara? Have you seen her recently?" asked Kent, hungry for more details. "It's been awhile since she's been here. Do you know why she hasn't been back?" his voice pleaded for answers.

They haven't heard about Tara's death. It shouldn't surprise me. Since it appeared to be an accident, the news made little of it. I bet what little coverage there was didn't make it to Cripple Creek. Ms. Hattie and Kent seem to be very genuine. Why was I hesitant to discuss Tara with them?

Feeling more comfortable than she had since she first arrived, but still a little cautious, Kelly proceeded to tell Kent and Hattie about her friend's "accident."

Chapter Fifteen

Kent appeared to be visibly shaken by the news of Tara. Hattie expressed sympathy, but no more than one would for someone they hardly knew. Considering how often Tara had visited, and how fond she had been of Hattie, Kelly felt hurt by Hattie's indifference. She observed the sorrow on Kent's face and wondered why he and Tara decided not to see each other anymore—at least on a personal level.

Kelly wondered if there was a reason Tara had stopped talking to her about the relationship. When she asked about it, Tara would only say that it never really got off the ground. She had wanted to discuss it more with Tara—and planned to—when they could meet some day for a long overdue lunch. But that day never came. Kelly always had the feeling that Kent meant a lot more to Tara than she wanted to admit. Now, looking at Kent, she had the sense that maybe he wasn't the one who wanted it to end. Then why *did* it end? That was the question Kelly kept asking herself ever since she met Kent. And it's one she hoped Tara would answer in her diary.

"Why is everyone so gloomy?" Robert asked as he entered the room. "The sun is out and bright enough to start melting the snow. You may be interested to know, I just heard they plan to begin clearing the roads as early as tomorrow."

Hattie spoke first. "Kelly has shared with us the most unfortunate news, Robert."

He went to the high-back chair where he normally sat. "Oh? And what might that be?" he asked, looking at Kelly.

"Robert, something dreadful has happened to Tara Medcalf," Hattie continued before Kelly could say anything. "You remember her, don't you...the friendly young lady who used to come visit us every couple of months?"

"Yes, I certainly remember Tara. She was as pretty a young lady as she was friendly. Did you say something happened to her?"

"She fell off a cliff while hiking," Hattie continued. "Isn't that correct, Kelly?"

"Yes. She was hiking on the Colorado National Monument over a trail she frequently used, and she got too close to the edge and lost her footing. She slipped and fell all the way to the bottom." Then Kelly added, as she fought back tears, "She died—thankfully, it was quick."

"How awful!" exclaimed Robert. "How did you find out about it, Kelly? Did you know Tara?"

"Kelly was Tara's friend," said Kent. "Kelly, are you the one who reported Tara missing?"

"No. I knew Tara was going hiking that Saturday. We last talked on the phone the night before. She asked if I wanted to come along. It was last minute, and I was obligated so I couldn't go. Sunday morning a hiker was walking the lower trail and noticed what he thought was a body on the canyon floor. He called 911."

"Did they do an autopsy, Kelly? Is it possible she could have had a medical problem that would have contributed to her falling?" questioned Kent. Then he whispered to himself, "Tara, I can't believe you're gone."

"They did perform an autopsy. There was nothing medically wrong with Tara that they could find." Kelly began to feel nervous. It was difficult talking about Tara with people she hardly knew, and she didn't want to indicate that she didn't believe it happened the way the police had said it did. "It was just a tragic, freak accident."

Once she had uttered those words, she felt a feeling of heaviness come over her. There was a pressure in her chest that she had never experienced before. She felt anxious, and smothered; she thought if she said one more word about Tara, she would not be able to take another breath. She had to change the subject.

"Robert, did you say they were going to clear the roads tomorrow?"

"That's my understanding. They are digging the snowplows out now and hope to work on the main streets as early as tomorrow morning. They may get to some of the side streets by tomorrow evening, but I wouldn't count on it. You learn when living in a small town, that there isn't the sense of urgency you'd find elsewhere."

"I suppose for some people that adds to its charm," added Kelly.

"Kelly, do you live in Denver?" asked Hattie

"No, I live in the Grand Valley on the Western Slope. Because of the energy boom, we've grown a lot in the last few years, but nowhere near the size of Denver or Colorado Springs."

Al walked in at the end of the conversation and gave his views on the virtues and pitfalls of a small town, so Tara's name never came up again. Kelly excused herself to go back to her room. Kent got up and followed her.

"Kelly, I'm really sorry about your friend, Tara."

"Yes, it's very sad." At that moment, she didn't want to talk about Tara anymore, and she was glad when she reached the stairs.

"Please wait," he said, as she put her foot on the step. "I'd like to talk to you if you have a few minutes."

"Kent, there you are!" interrupted Hattie. "I forgot to tell you, I need your help with some boxes in the kitchen."

"Mother, I don't recall seeing any boxes."

"Of course you don't. They weren't there when you were in the kitchen. I dragged them out of the pantry to look for some spices I had packed when I put up the patio dishes last fall. You know which ones, the spices that we usually use when we cook out on the grill. Since Kelly has the misfortune of being stranded here, I have a special dish I'd like to make for her tonight, and it calls for one of the spices. I strained my back when I got one of the boxes off the shelf looking for it. I don't dare try to put them back by myself."

Kelly watched Kent as his mother spoke. It seemed by his body language that he didn't believe her story.

"Maybe we can talk later, Kelly."

"Okay," she said, then realized she was almost disappointed.

"I'm sorry to put you through so much trouble, Ms. Hattie. I know you usually don't serve dinner to guests. A sandwich would have been fine with me."

"Nonsense, it's no trouble at all, dear—I look forward to it."

Kelly wasn't sure she meant it, but deep down she hoped that she did. She was having conflicting feelings about Hattie and it bothered her. She watched as Kent followed her into the kitchen. *What did he want to talk to me about? Was it Tara, or something else?*

Chapter Sixteen

Subdued, she lay across the bed and thought about Tara. She wished she had been more involved in her life the last few years. Maybe if she had gone hiking with her, Tara would still be alive. She wept and thought about the ritual she and Tara had performed at age ten when they decided to become blood sisters.

"Come on, Kelly," urged Tara, "it won't hurt, and when it's over, we'll be sisters forever!"

"I know. I'm not afraid; I was just wondering what we were going to use to cut ourselves," exclaimed Kelly.

"Follow me. I have everything set up in the play-house."

Tara ran towards the backyard at such a fast pace, Kelly had a hard time catching up. But when Tara got to the opened door of the playhouse, Kelly was right on her heels.

"Wow," said Kelly as she looked in and saw an old crate in the middle of the room. It reminded her of a surgeon's cart prepared for surgery. There was a bottle of alcohol, cotton balls, a needle, Band-Aids, knife, and a lit candle, all neatly arranged on a clean towel.

"Why a knife?" asked Kelly.

"Oh, that's only in case we can't get enough blood from the needle. I don't think we'll need it, but we have to make sure there's enough to mix together so we'll really be sisters."

Tara reached for the bottle of alcohol, and a cotton ball, then began to explain the procedure to Kelly as she went through each step. Kelly marveled at how much alike they were. Usually, she was in charge of setting things up, but this time, Tara insisted that she be in charge because she was the oldest, even if it was by only two days.

"Give me your finger," said Tara as she poured alcohol on the cotton ball. "My mom says alcohol kills germs. She always uses it on my dad when he gets cuts and scratches." When she finished rubbing the alcohol on Kelly's finger, she did her own, then reached for the needle. First she stuck herself, because she knew she was braver than Kelly, and then she stuck Kelly. Kelly held her breath and closed her eyes. When she felt the prick she opened her eyes; she was pleased with herself that she didn't flinch. They both began squeezing their fingers, and when they had enough blood bubbling up, they put them together and at the same time said...

"Sisters forever!"

They quickly put Band-Aids on so they could keep each other's blood inside. It wasn't until then that Tara realized she'd forgotten to put the needle over the flame of the candle. Years later, they would laugh at how they worried for weeks that one or both would get an infection.

But that was then, and it was a long time ago, and she wanted her best friend back. She wanted to redo the last few years and spend more time with her. She wiped her tears, sat up on the bed, and grabbed her cell phone off the nightstand. She needed to talk to someone. She called Stan.

"Hello, Kelly. I wondered when I'd hear from you. Are you rich yet?" he joked.

"Funny, Stan. You know I don't like to gamble. Although I will say, if Ms. Hattie had machines in this place, I might take it up. I'm going stir-crazy."

"I'm sure you are, Kelly. You don't function well unless you're working with a full plate—or at least your own schedule. Seriously, how are you doing in captivity?"

"Something doesn't feel right, Stan. I know that sounds silly. And maybe it's only because I had expected it to be different, but the atmosphere around here is not comfortable, like I thought it would be."

"What did you expect?"

"I'm not sure. In the beginning, Tara used to talk so fondly of this place—and of Ms. Hattie. But she didn't talk much about Cripple Creek the last few months of her life—it seemed we both were so busy then. Or maybe it was because she had tried to get me to go with her on several occasions, but I was the one who was always too busy. She eventually quit asking. When we did find time to talk, we spent most of it just catching up on work, friends, and relatives. I don't know, Stan—for the most part, everyone here is pleasant and friendly, but something feels strange."

"Kelly, you really do need to get out and travel more. I'm sure it took Tara a few visits before she felt totally comfortable. And I'm sure she wasn't confined due to a blizzard like you are."

"That's true. Maybe it's nothing more than my own restlessness."

"Try to relax, read a book, and take advantage of the situation."

"I'm trying, but I'd like to get out of here for awhile and explore the rest of the town." She didn't tell Stan about Tara's diary or about the shadows at her door. But she did tell him that she was convinced Tara had met with foul play.

"Kelly, I was hoping by getting away you would have a chance to properly grieve Tara and accept that she is gone. What is, is. You can't change it."

"I know I can't bring Tara back, but I owe it to her to find out what happened. I've been thinking about the police report. I was too much in shock at the time of her death and accepted—along with everyone else—that it was an accident. It wasn't until several weeks later that I started having second thoughts. In the report, the police ruled it an accident because it had begun to rain close to the time they estimated she had fallen. They speculated that the ground might have been wet, and the rocks near the edge of the cliff where she supposedly fell, could have been slippery. Stan, you were with me when I talked to the detective. Didn't he say that by the time they found her body it had been raining hard?"

"Yes, he did say that. What's your point?"

"If Tara encountered a problem with someone, while the ground was still reasonably dry, they could have dragged her to the edge and pushed her. If this happened when it first started to rain, then there would have been footprints, and the heavy rains that came later could have washed them away."

"Kelly, I have given some thought to this since our last conversation about Tara, so I'll indulge you—for awhile. If someone murdered Tara, what was the motive? She wasn't raped. She never carried money on her when she hiked—according to you—so we can rule out robbery. She didn't have an enemy—at least that we know of. And no one on the trail that day remembered seeing anyone who looked suspicious. If you're going to explore this any further, you have to find a motive."

"I know, I know." Kelly was silent for a moment, and then asked, "What if Tara saw, or overheard, something she wasn't supposed to? Maybe someone didn't deliberately target her, but she got in the way."

"Now you're going out on a limb. What could Tara possibly have seen, or heard, on a hiking trail that would have endangered her life?"

"Okay, Stan, I see your point. It's not your typical place to plan a murder, or a drug deal, or map out a bank robbery. But something did happen to Tara on that trail to cause her death, other than slipping on wet rocks and falling off the cliff. I have to find out what really happened to her, Stan, and all I ask is that you keep an open mind. I need to talk about this, and right now you're the only one I can call. I know the more I talk about it, and analyze the possibilities, something is apt to come to me."

"Okay, Kelly, I'll keep an open mind, on one condition…"

"What's that?"

"Don't cloud your judgment by becoming obsessed. And remember what I've always preached to you before allowing anything to be put in print."

Kelly knew the rules all too well and played them over in her mind. *Check out the credibility and reliability of your source. Research the facts and any other information to validate its authenticity before you accept that it is accurate. And always keep your emotions separate—don't rush to judgment in order to prove your theory.*

"I'm afraid you don't have anything to go on, Kelly— and you're too close to the situation."

"That's why I need your help," she said. She knew Stan had friends in the police department. One of his buddies was with the Colorado Bureau of Investigation. "The police weren't looking for anything suspicious when they investigated," she continued. "The scene was too clean. But, Stan, if you could review their report, with a suspicious mind, maybe you would find something worth looking into."

"I'll talk with you about it when you get back, Kelly. Put it to rest for now and try to enjoy your vacation." He changed the subject and went on to ask about the weather, how soon the roads would be cleared, and now that she had been detained, where she was going next.

Kelly smiled when the call was over. She felt a small sense of accomplishment. For the first time, she had actually engaged Stan in more than a two-minute conversation as to how Tara died. He told her to put it to rest and enjoy her vacation, but she knew she couldn't do that. She didn't know where she'd go when she left Cripple Creek, if anywhere. All she knew at that moment was that she had the need to delve deeper into Tara's diary. And where better to do it than in Cripple Creek?

Chapter Seventeen

Hattie had proven her meal would be special—dinner was excellent. And once Kelly asked about the mining industry, there wasn't a lack for conversation. Robert and Al were very sociable. Robert even teased Kelly, telling her that he and Al weren't privy to such gourmet meals when she wasn't there. Over all, with only one exception, the evening couldn't have been more pleasant. But Kelly wished Hattie and Kent would have joined them for dinner.

Robert and Al had been boarders for many years—they were more like family—and yet Hattie and Kent ate with them only on holidays. Robert said it was because he and Al liked to eat early, around 6 p.m. Hattie and Kent usually ate between 7:30 and 8 p.m.

Kelly lay across the bed and thought about the evening. It was very pleasant. She was surprised, though, that she didn't see Kent. Even if he did eat later, she felt it would have been a good opportunity to discuss what he had wanted to talk to her about earlier that day—unless he preferred not having Robert or Al present.

She thought about everything that had taken place the last two days. The drive to Cripple Creek, the people she met, the conversations that were held, and the shadows at her door at four in the morning. She was analytical by nature, but now she wanted to dissect every aspect of her trip—and this time, she hadn't forgotten to secure the door for the night. Kelly knew she wasn't ready to leave Cripple Creek. Even as much as she wanted to go, she felt compelled to stay.

Since Tara had stayed at Dolly's, Kelly wondered if she had met Ed—and if she had, would he remember her. Maybe she would have mentioned him in her diary. Kelly was tempted to skim through the pages, but she wanted to experience the love Tara had for Cripple Creek page by page. She wanted to understand why the connection happened. Was it the town, the people, gambling, or something else that kept bringing Tara back? Kelly didn't want to rush through the pages like she had rushed through life the past five years. Tara's death was sudden, and it occurred almost 300 miles from Cripple Creek. Kelly didn't know how Tara died; she just knew she couldn't accept that it was accidental. But she knew it didn't make sense: everyone liked Tara, and she gave no indication that she had any concern for her life. Maybe she just happened to be at the wrong place at the wrong time. Could a deranged person have taken his or her anger out on Tara? Kelly wondered if her questions would ever be answered. What really *did* happen? She sighed, then picked up the diary.

The last entry she had read was from March twenty-second. Two weeks had passed before Tara wrote again. Her next entry began...

April 6th, *Hi, Friend—it's been awhile since I've written. I broke my commitment of three times a week. Sometimes everyday life gets in the way. It's funny I should say that—after all, life means living, and I don't feel I've done much of that lately. I did go to Cripple Creek again last weekend with Shelly. We stayed at Dolly's Silver Lining Casino. I don't know, I guess I'm not the gambler that Shelly is. She can play non-stop, but after awhile, I'm bored. We did go up and down the streets and visited several other casinos. It's interesting how they can differ and still be so much alike. We passed an antique shop and a couple of quaint gift shops. I did enjoy browsing through those. Actually, I guess I did have a good time. I'm just feeling melancholy this morning.*

Something interesting happened the last night we were there. After dinner, Shelly and I sat at the bar and played video poker while we had a drink. Both bartenders were very friendly. They'd stop by and chat in between serving other patrons. Of course, Shelly is so outgoing, and maybe they wouldn't have spent as much time if I had been there by myself. Ed, one of the bartenders, had a friend stop by, and he happened to sit next to me. He and Ed talked back and forth for awhile, and then Ed introduced him to Shelly and me. His name is Kent, and, boy, is he good looking! What's interesting is, he and his mother run a small bed-and-breakfast a few blocks down the street from Dolly's. He gave us both a card and suggested Shelly and I try their place next time we come. Ed gave him a hard time about taking business away from Dolly's, but it was all in jest. I won't be able to go back to Cripple Creek until June. The card says, Ms. Hattie's Bed & Breakfast. I think I'll give it a try.

Kelly, I need to call you this week and fill you in. You always keep me grounded. Maybe I'm feeling melancholy because I would like the opportunity to learn more about Kent. But he's probably married. Aside from being the best-looking man in the place, he seemed genuinely nice, but all the nice ones are taken.

Kelly continued...reading until she reached the middle of May. She had read about the time when Tara called her and filled her in on the first time she met Kent. The rest of the entries were mostly about work and hiking. *So Tara did meet Ed! I don't remember her mentioning him to me, but it's been so long ago that I guess I forgot. I'm sure Ed would remember her, especially if he introduced her to Kent.*

Kelly was anxious to get to the month of June, and she would have read more that night, but she felt queasy. She put the diary down and thought about Hattie's dinner. *I know better than to eat too much of a good thing. If I had only eaten half the amount of the chicken dish, or not taken so much, I would have been okay. It was so delicious I hated to stop, but I know my digestive system can't handle a sauce as rich as the one the chicken was smothered in.* She looked in her purse for the Tums. There weren't any to be found. Then she remembered she had taken the last one before she left home and had forgotten to put another pack in her purse. "Damn," she said out loud, "that's what I get for not making a list and waiting until the last minute to pack." She climbed in bed and tried to fall asleep, but the nausea worsened. She tossed back and forth as she tried to get comfortable. Not even the Tums would have helped. She knew she was going to lose that wonderful meal. She rolled out of bed and grabbed the wastebasket in case it was needed before the bathroom was reached.

It had been awhile since Kelly had felt that sick. She had been in the bathroom for almost an hour. When she got back to the room, she crawled into bed—better, but weak—and wanted nothing more than to sleep. But the harder she tried, the more awake she became…and she felt Tara's presence. It was almost eerie. Then she remembered when she was at the funeral, she'd had a similar feeling. At first she brushed it off. *Tara, I have too much time on my hands. I'm tired, weak, and I'm missing you. I don't know why, but I feel you here tonight. Did you stay in this room when you were here? I'm weary—but I can't sleep. I can't get you off my mind.* She turned towards the wall, away from the nightstand; but when she did, a strong urge came over her to turn back towards it. She did, and without thinking, she sat up and reached for the light. The diary! It wasn't faceup like she had left it. A chill went through her. She knew she didn't leave it that way. It was a pet peeve of hers. She hated for any book to be placed facedown.

Kelly got out of bed and looked around. Had anything else been touched or moved? She couldn't tell. Everything else—her suitcase and the furniture—appeared the same as when she left the room. Locking the door was not a priority when she felt ill and rushed to the bathroom. A host of questions went through her head: Why would someone have come into her room? Did she leave the door open? Even if she had, that wouldn't give anyone the right to just walk in. *Maybe whoever came in thought I purposely left the door open and they were welcome. But when they saw I wasn't here, they should have left. How dare someone touch Tara's diary! How dare they pick it up!* Then she felt a tremendous concern. Did someone have the audacity to look through it? She felt violated, and even worse, she felt she had let Tara down. *Oh, Tara, I am so sorry*, she thought. *This will not happen again. No matter what happens, I'll lock the door!*

Kelly wasn't weak anymore. And she wasn't scared. She was angry! She put her robe and slippers on and went into the hallway. She looked across the hall from where she stood. The doors to rooms 3 and 4 were still open and, of course, no one had checked in. The lights were still off in both rooms. She wondered if anyone was hiding in either one. She walked across the hall and went into room 4. After she checked it out she went down the hall to room 3. Both rooms were similar to the one she was staying in, and both were empty. She came out of room 3 and looked across the hall to Al's room. It was late, but she could tell he had the light on. Since the hall light was dimmer than the light in the room, and the door was about an inch off the floor, there was no mistaking the light was on.

Kelly wanted to knock on his door and ask if he had been in her room. But if he had, and if he had touched the diary—or worse yet, looked through it—he wouldn't admit it. And then he would suspect that she knew what he had done. Al? She couldn't imagine he would have had any reason to enter her room. She felt defeated and headed back. She had taken only two steps when Al opened his door.

"Kelly?" he was surprised to see her there.

Her face flushed, but she tried to act nonchalant.

"Hi, Al. I guess this makes two of us that can't sleep. I was restless and thought I'd walk the hall a few times. Considering how much I ate for dinner, I'm hoping the exercise will do me some good. What keeps you up this late, or are you normally a night owl?"

"No, I'm not usually a night owl. I was going to take a shower earlier, but I guess you were in the bathroom. I waited awhile, but I know how you women are. I came back to the room and watched TV. I guess I fell asleep. I just woke up and decided I'd better get in the shower now so I wouldn't bother you in the morning."

Kelly felt she should apologize, but she didn't want to. She wasn't sure that Al hadn't been the one in her room, and if he was, he didn't deserve the apology—she did.

"It's all yours, Al. I'm going to bed." She turned briskly and left.

When she got to the room, she made sure the door was locked behind her, and then got into bed. *If not Al, then who?* she wondered. *Kent wanted to talk to me this afternoon. I didn't see him at dinner. Could he have come looking for me, saw the door open, and walked in? Maybe he came in, and when I wasn't here he turned to leave, but then noticed the diary. When he saw it was Tara's, he couldn't resist looking through it.*

Or maybe he picked it up not knowing what it was, and when he realized it was a diary, quickly put it back, but in his haste placed it facedown.

Kelly didn't know what to think. She didn't have anyone to talk to. Stan was too far away, and there was no reason to worry him anyway. As she drifted off, she thought about Joe. Ed had told her that Joe was a straight shooter. He also said Joe came to Cripple Creek every few months. Was it only to gamble, or did he have other reasons? That cup of coffee was sounding good...

Chapter Eighteen

He wakened to the sound of snowplows. Eight-thirty in the morning, and he was still in bed. But then it had been half-past four before he fell asleep. The room was a mess, papers everywhere, but at least he felt he had made *some* progress. He sat on the edge of the bed, yawned, and appraised the mess before him.

Joe was not used to sleeping in. It made him edgy. He got up and looked through the paperwork of Tiffany Buckley's strewn file. He had highlighted everything pertaining to Jason Goldbloom. He knew he was onto something. Someone had used Goldbloom's name and personal information to set up the appointment with Tiffany. Jason Goldbloom lived in St. Louis. He only came to Colorado Springs to design a golf course, and that was the year before Tiffany was murdered. When he was in Colorado Springs, he stayed at the Marriott Hotel. Then the weekend before he left to go home, he visited Cripple Creek and stayed at Dolly's.

Tiffany was last seen alive in Cripple Creek. Joe had focused his investigation on the stolen identity of Jason Goldbloom in Colorado Springs. He was only drawn to Cripple Creek because Tiffany was last seen alive here.

Last night, he finally had an epiphany: What if Jason Goldbloom's identity had been stolen when he was in Cripple Creek? Or whoever killed Tiffany had remembered him from the year before and figured no one would connect the dots? If that was the case, then someone in Cripple Creek had to have gotten Goldbloom's information from when he checked in at Dolly's.

Martha was usually at the desk during the time of check-in. Joe wondered how easy it would have been for someone to gain access to the guests' information. Everything was on computer now, not like the old hand-written system that places used to use.

Jason Goldbloom had been in Cripple Creek during one weekend only, and he never returned. If he paid by credit card, like he did in Colorado Springs, Dolly's would have had a record of it, but considering how long it had been, the records may have been purged. If he had a drink at the bar or ate in the cafe and used his credit card, someone could have gained access to his ID through his credit card information. Joe wondered if anyone who had worked at Dolly's six years ago, other than Martha, would still be here. He needed a cup of coffee, and he wanted to talk to Carla.

"Well, aren't we late for our java jolt this morning," Carla announced in a sarcastic tone when she saw Joe.

"Are you always this pleasant?" he responded.

"No, sometimes I'm crabby. What'll it be, just coffee—or do you want toast with it?"

"Bring me a menu. I'm hungry this morning."

"Will do," said Carla, who left abruptly.

Joe tried to remember if she had waited on him during one of his past trips, but to his recollection, the first time he'd ever seen her was at dinner the other night when he and Kelly were there together. He couldn't imagine that if she *had* waited on him before, he wouldn't remember her. And the only time he knew of her name was when Kelly read it off her name tag.

Carla was soon back. "I brought coffee with the menu. You look like you could use some."

She was right: Joe looked a mess. He was anxious to get downstairs so he didn't bother shaving, and he barely took a comb to his hair.

"What's your special this morning?" he asked.

"Don't have one, but I always recommend the ham steak and eggs. Can't go wrong with it."

"Okay, that sounds good. I'll have it." He handed her the menu, then asked, "Carla, have you noticed the streets are being cleared?" He decided he'd try to get her in a better mood before he asked the questions he really wanted to.

"They're trying, at least," she replied, "but Cripple Creek could use some new equipment. What little they have is outdated."

"Have you lived in Cripple Creek most of your life?"

"Nope, only been here a few years."

"How long have you been working at Dolly's?"

"Do you want to chitchat or would you rather I put this order in before they start serving lunch?" she said curtly, but then added a half smile.

"I guess you'd better put the order in. I'm hungry for breakfast." He figured he'd better take it slow. Carla had a curious nature, and if she knew anything, he didn't want her suspicious of him. She was different, that's for sure. He was determined not to let her get to him.

When his breakfast came, it wasn't Carla who brought it, but the other waitress—whom he assumed was Tonya. She wasn't wearing a name tag, but he remembered Carla mentioning that she would be the other person working until more help could come in and relieve them.

"Carla got tied up in the kitchen and asked me to bring your order. Do you need anything else right now?" she asked.

"Maybe some more coffee when you get a chance." As she left, he wondered which one would come back with the coffee. Was it just coincidental, or was Carla avoiding him? Since the kitchen was shorthanded, he knew they needed her help at times, but the cafe wasn't busy. The lunch crowd hadn't begun to appear. It seemed only seconds had passed when Tonya returned with the coffee. Joe seized the opportunity.

"It looks like you may get lucky today. If they keep working on the roads, you and Carla might make it home tonight."

"Oh, man, I hope so! It's been a tough couple of days," Tonya said, rolling her tired shoulders.

"Have you ever experienced anything like this before?" asked Joe.

"Not that I remember—not like this, anyway. I've been living here going on five years, and this is the worst I've seen. Even Carla said the most snow she remembers Cripple Creek getting was a foot and a half—maybe two feet at the most—and she's been here a few years longer than I have. She usually works the dinner shift, and she's never had a problem getting home before. I haven't worked at Dolly's as long as she has, and I'm generally leaving when her shift begins." Tonya looked up and saw several people enter the cafe. "I'd better get going. I think our stranded guests are running out of gambling money. They seem to be coming in for lunch a little earlier than usual." She left the coffeepot with Joe and went to greet them.

That was a worthwhile conversation, he thought. *Carla told me she lived in Cripple Creek for only a few years. Tonya's been here for five years and she says Carla's been here a few years longer than that. Why did Carla tell me she's only been here a few years? Was it intentional for some reason, or just a figure of speech? Based on what Tonya said, I figure Carla's been in Cripple Creek eight to ten years. That's more than a few years. And I know why I didn't recognize her; I've never eaten dinner at Dolly's before this trip. Why was she being evasive? Is she suspicious of me, or afraid I'll become suspicious of her?*

Chapter Nineteen

After the night she had had, breakfast didn't sound good, but Kelly decided to go down and at least make an appearance. She told Hattie she was still full from the night before and asked only for tea and toast. Everything seemed normal. There was no indication that anyone had been in her room. She wondered if it could have been possible that she inadvertently laid the diary facedown. She couldn't imagine having done so, but then, she *was* ill.

She finished the tea and toast and retreated to the parlor before going back to her room. She was standing at the window when Kent walked in.

"Do you see the plows yet?" he asked.

"I hear them, but I don't see them yet," she said as she turned to face him. "Kent, you said you wanted to talk to me. Is this a good time?"

"Perhaps," he sat down and Kelly joined him. "I hope you don't mind my asking about Tara, but I was curious to know how well you knew her."

"No, I don't mind." She took a deep breath, let it out, then proceeded. "Tara and I were childhood friends. During our college years we went our separate ways, but we always kept in touch. Our careers took different paths, so we didn't spend as much time together as we would have liked."

Kelly didn't want him to know that, at the ages of ten, she and Tara became blood sisters; that as they grew to adulthood, there was very little one didn't know about the other. She didn't want him to know that part of her died when Tara's life ended. She wasn't sure how much she wanted to tell him, but she felt she'd said enough. She also didn't want Kent to know Tara had talked to her about him—at least not yet.

Kent didn't respond right away; he just sat there in thought.

"Why do you ask, Kent?" she inquired.

"No reason in particular." He paused, then looked straight into her eyes. "Well, that's not exactly true. Kelly, I was very fond of Tara. She was a wonderful person. She used to come here a lot. I have no idea why she quit coming to Cripple Creek, and I certainly didn't know about her accident." He looked away towards the window, if for only a moment, and then continued. "I didn't know she died. Tara and I enjoyed spending time together. We really became good friends. She was coming here about every two months, and there were times we even arranged to meet at a different location. Once, she talked me into joining her on the Colorado National Monument and we hiked together. After you told us about what happened to her, I haven't been able to get her off my mind. When I stopped you at the stairs, I wanted to ask if you knew why she had quit coming. I was hoping she might have told you."

If Kent had been the one in Kelly's room, she was sure he didn't read through the diary, or he would have known Tara had talked to her about him. And when he looked her in the eyes, she could see how genuine he was—how much he cared about Tara—and she felt only compassion for him.

"Kent, I can honestly say, that I don't know why Tara quit coming to Cripple Creek. There were times when she mentioned how much she enjoyed coming here, but for the last several months—just prior to her death— the subject never came up."

He leaned back in his chair and gave a defeated sigh. Then, without looking at Kelly, he asked, "Did she ever mention my name?"

She waited before answering, weighing her words carefully. She would have liked to have shared with him how fondly Tara talked about him and how much she cared, but she still wasn't sure if she could fully trust him. She wanted to...and she couldn't imagine Kent being at her door at four in the morning, or in her room touching Tara's diary; but she knew someone had, and as much as she wanted to, she wasn't ready to trust anyone. Something about Ms. Hattie's Bed & Breakfast was very different for Kelly from the way Tara experienced it. She wondered if Tara had felt the difference towards the end, and maybe that was why she didn't mention Cripple Creek anymore. And could it be possible that that was why she stopped seeing Kent?

She was reserved when she answered. "I do remember Tara mentioning someone named Kent." Before she could say anymore, she heard Robert. He had a book in his hand, and even though the sofa was unoccupied, he looked as if there was no place to sit. Kelly realized that she was using what seemed to be his chair.

"Here, Robert—you can sit here. I was just leaving," she said when she got out of the chair.

"There's no need to leave on my account. I suppose I could sit on the sofa."

"No really, Robert, you can sit here. I'm going to make a phone call and then try to finish a book I've started. It doesn't look as though the snowplows will get to the side roads today, so I might as well take advantage of the time I have." She looked at Kent and knew by the look on his face, that he had wanted to hear more. But since Robert was there, he seemed resigned to end the conversation.

"Thank you, Kelly. I do hope I'm not rushing you off," Robert said as he sat down in his favorite chair.

"Not at all; please enjoy your day. I'm sure I'll be seeing you later." She left and went upstairs. She wanted to call Dolly's to see if they had cleared Main Street and to check on her car.

"Hello, Dolly's Silver Lining Casino," answered a woman with a soft-spoken voice, "Martha speaking."

"Hello, Martha, this is Kelly Murphy. I drove into Cripple Creek the other day during the snowstorm. I'm staying at Ms. Hattie's B & B, but I had to leave my car parked in front of Dolly's. Could you tell me if Main Street has been cleared yet?"

"Let's just say they made an attempt. The drifts made it more difficult to plow, and the stranded cars didn't help. I hate to tell you this, but if your car was parked out front, it's probably buried worse now than it was before."

"Oh gee, I was afraid of that. Martha, you don't think they'll tow it away, do you?"

"Not without giving you a chance to move it first. I think they'll be back later this afternoon and try to finish clearing. Some of the casino workers are shoveling the sidewalks and out around the cars. The sun has been bright today and the temperature is above freezing, so that should help. There's just so much snow, it's a slow process."

"Do you know if they will get to any of the side streets today?" Kelly asked.

"I'm not sure. But if they can, it will probably be the ones around the casinos."

Kelly thought about Joe. He might have his car dug out by tonight and could possibly be able to leave sometime tomorrow. The streets around Hattie's would still be unplowed. It seemed crazy, but she had a strong sense that she should talk to him.

"Martha, if you have the time, could I trouble you for another moment?"

"This is actually a good time. What can I help you with?"

"You have a guest staying with you who I believe comes every few months. I met him the other night. I'm supposed to have coffee with him before I leave town, but

I'm afraid I won't make it up there before he's ready to leave. I'd like to leave him a message, but I don't know his last name. His first name is Joe. I know that's not much to go on..."

Martha cut in before Kelly could finish. "You're in luck! We only have a few rooms here at Dolly's, and I only have one Joe staying here. You must be talking about Joe Conrad. I'll leave him a message if you'd like, but why don't I try his room first?"

Kelly hesitated, then said, "Okay." Martha rang Joe's room but there was no answer. Kelly left a message—and at the last second, she decided to leave her cell number.

Chapter Twenty

Since Kelly had returned to her room, she had been absorbed with Tara's diary. It was the second week of June before Tara made a visit back to Cripple Creek, and it was also the first time she stayed at Ms. Hattie's. At the last minute, Shelly had had unexpected company and couldn't go.

She had finally gotten to the entry of June twelfth when her phone rang. She assumed it was Stan.

"You're a hard one to buy a cup of coffee for."

She recognized Joe's voice. "I'm often told I can be difficult. I appreciate the offer, Joe, but it doesn't look like I was meant to have that cup of coffee. It also looks like you could be leaving and on your way home as early as tomorrow, and I'll be lucky if they even begin digging me out by then. That's why I left the message. I didn't want you waiting around for me to show up."

"Well actually, Kelly, I've decided to stick around for a couple more days. Main Street's looking pretty good; they've been working on it all day. But I still have to drive down a mountain road to Divide. I'm sure by now the road's okay through Woodland Park to Colorado Springs, but getting to that point might be tricky. I hate to admit it, but I'm a nervous driver on snow-packed roads."

"You don't strike me as the nervous type, Joe, but if and when I ever get out of here, I'll let you know."

"Kelly, why don't you call me once the road is cleared, and I'll come down and get you? You're probably anxious to get your car, and I really think by tomorrow, the snowplows will make it down your way."

She was quiet. She questioned the idea of getting in a car with someone she barely knew, and yet, part of her felt as though she did know him.

He broke the silence. "Kelly, believe me, I'm harmless. Ask Ed, the bartender—he'll vouch for me."

"I'm sure you are, Joe. And at this point, I'll take my chances. I'm not used to being confined this long—I'm going stir-crazy."

"Write down my cell number. As soon as they clear the road in front of Ms. Hattie's, give me a call."

She wrote down the number and told him she would call. She hung up and looked at the clock: she had an hour before dinner. She opened the diary and continued.

June 12th, _Hi, Friend—I had a great weekend! Went to Cripple Creek and stayed at Ms. Hattie's Bed & Breakfast. What an experience! I really like the place. It's an old Victorian home that was converted into a boardinghouse/bed-and-breakfast. I stayed upstairs in room 2. It was very comfortable._

At first, I felt uneasy going by myself, but now I'm glad I did. If Shelly had been with me, we would have gone straight down-

town to the casinos and probably stayed there until late evening. I wouldn't have had the chance to get to know Kent. As it was, I only saw him twice. But both times we spent about an hour talking. He is very nice, good-looking, and available. At least I think he's available. He mentioned he was divorced but didn't say whether or not he had a significant other. He did ask when I'd be coming back. I had told Shelly this would be my last time until next year. Since I'm not the gambler she is, I'd rather be hiking. But when Kent asked, I found myself saying I'd be back in two or three months. I couldn't believe I said it, but I did. Now I'm thinking that I really want to go back—and sometime soon. There seemed to be chemistry between Kent and me—at least I thought there was. I hope he felt it, too. It's been awhile since I've allowed myself to get interested in any-one—seriously interested, that is, but I feel that's about to change! I've enjoyed going out with Jack and Pete. They've been very good friends, but I've known all along neither one wants to settle down. I guess I haven't been ready either—that's probably why I like being with them.

Kent is different. He seems to have more of a serious, thoughtful side...not at all the playboy run-around type. I can tell he has a fun side, but in a good way. I better not wait too long before going back or he might meet someone else. I'll check my date book tomorrow. Even if I can't go back for two or three months, if I at least call and make reservations, he'll know I'm coming. I don't think I'll tell Shelly I'm going. I will tell Kelly—I have to tell Kelly! But I'm not even going to invite her this time. It would be the one time she'd decide to come, and I want to get to know Kent on my own. But Kelly, as always, I will fill you in.

Kelly smiled. Tara had stayed in the same room she was in.

It was almost six o'clock; Kelly didn't want to be late for dinner. As it was, Ms. Hattie was being generous to include her. She closed the diary and buried it under her nightgown at the bottom of her suitcase. She never did unpack it—she wanted to be ready to leave at a moment's notice. She looked in the mirror above the wooden table. She was wearing the last clean outfit she had with her. The rest of her clothes were in the other suitcase that she left in the car. *Maybe if I wear the blouse I wore the first day with the pants I wore yesterday, no one will realize I'm wearing dirty clothes.* She decided that would work for the time being and hoped she'd be able to get her car by tomorrow. Then she wondered: Once she had her car, would she be satisfied staying at Ms. Hattie's? Would she transfer to Dolly's? Or would she leave Cripple Creek, head home, and give up on her vacation?

On the way to the dining room, she thought about all of her options. She told herself that she would wait until after dinner to make a decision. But by the time she had reached the bottom step, part of her decision had been settled. She was convinced; leaving Cripple Creek early was not an option. She didn't pretend to understand why, and it didn't make sense. But she knew she had to stay awhile longer.

Chapter Twenty-One

"There she is," said Robert as Kelly sat down at the dining room table. "I was beginning to wonder if you had sequestered yourself for the rest of the evening. We missed you in the parlor this afternoon. Hattie made blueberry scones, and they were wonderful with the blackberry tea she prepared."

"I'm sorry I missed out. I'm sure I would have enjoyed them."

"That must be some book you're reading."

"Book?" Kelly repeated in a puzzled tone. As far as she knew, he couldn't have meant the diary, and that was the only book she had been reading.

"Yes. You said this morning when you left the parlor that you were going upstairs to read a good book you had brought. I assumed this afternoon that you must be in the midst of it. I know when I'm deep in the middle of a good book, I lose all track of time."

"You're absolutely right, Robert. I had forgotten about mentioning the book to you." She had gathered her thoughts quickly and felt she was back in control.

"So tell me, Kelly, what type of reading do you enjoy?"

Al broke in, "Maybe she doesn't want you to know what kind of books she likes to read."

"Oh really, Al, I'm not being intrusive. I'm just interested. Being an avid reader myself, Kelly, I'm always fascinated by what others find interesting. I hope you don't mind my asking."

"Not at all," she said, then hoped he didn't ask for the name of the book. She liked Robert. He was well-mannered and always polite—a true gentleman. "Actually, my favorite books are biographies. I enjoy reading how someone else has lived their life; the hardships, failures, triumphs, and successes. Everyone has a story to tell. I believe we can all benefit from their experiences. What do you like to read, Robert?"

"My interests are somewhat in the same vein as yours. I am a true history buff, but I must say, I also love a good classic. I can get lost in a good piece of literature, such as *Pride and Prejudice*, *Moby Dick*, and *Gone with the Wind*, to name a few. I also like the lighter fare as well, and I enjoy everything by Charles Dickens."

Hattie was later than usual serving dinner, but she finally made her entrance before Kelly had a chance to respond.

"I'm running a little late. I apologize. I was tied up on the phone with my sister from New York. I hadn't spoken to her for months until this storm, and she has called twice in the last few days. Isn't it ironic that it should take inclement weather to raise the concern for one's family? I guess people are just too busy these days to care like they should." She set down a platter of pot roast surrounded by potatoes and carrots.

When Hattie returned to the kitchen for the rolls, Kelly thought about her own sister, Sara. Since their parents' deaths, the only time she kept in touch with Sara was during holidays, birthdays, and a response to an occasional e-mail Sara would send. She felt she hardly knew her niece and nephew—and she realized it was her fault, not Sara's. Sara made the attempt, but Kelly stayed too busy. *Where has my life gone? I've lost my marriage, my parents, my best friend, and I don't even keep in touch with the only family I have left—Sara, Todd, Rebecca and Josh.*

"Kelly, are you alright?" Al asked as he held the platter before her. She didn't seem to notice it at first.

"She's thinking about all the wonderful books I've read," Robert teased.

"Thank you, Al," she said, and scooped some meat and vegetables onto her plate. "My mind did wander a moment. I was thinking about Ms. Hattie's phone call from her sister. It reminded me that I need to call *my* sister.

"You have a sister, Kelly? How nice. I don't have any siblings, but I always wished I did," remarked Robert. "Are you and your sister close?"

"Not as close as we used to be—as I'd *like* to be— but I'm going to work on that when I get back home." She turned to Al. "What about you, Al—do you have any brothers or sisters?"

"I have an older sister living in Kansas City. We write to each other, and once a year we take turns visiting. We spend about a week together. I guess we're as close as two people can be, but after a week together, we're ready to be on our way. I don't have any brothers. Maybe that's why Robert and I like living at Hattie's. Here, we're like family." He turned back to his food and continued eating.

After the main course, Hattie came back with a devil's food cake. Kent was right behind her with the plates and forks. Everyone was surprised when Hattie and Kent sat down and joined them for dessert.

"Hattie, did you have an earlier dinner than usual, or did you decide to forego dinner in favor of this fabulous-looking dessert?"

"Actually, Robert, Kent and I had a very late lunch. Most times I try not to eat desserts, but since devil's food cake is my favorite, I decided to skip dinner and join everyone for dessert instead." She began to cut the cake and handed the first piece to Kelly.

"I told Mother I liked her idea. If I get hungry later, I can always make a sandwich. Besides," Kent said as he looked at Kelly, "this might be Kelly's last night here. The side streets should be cleared by tomorrow afternoon. I'm sure you'll be anxious to be on your way."

Everyone looked in Kelly's direction. She was about to speak when Robert spoke up. "Kelly, will you continue on to Santa Fe?"

"I'm not sure, but I doubt it. The first thing at the top of my priority list will be to get my car. Then I'll try to figure out what I'm going to do next. Now that I'm here in Cripple Creek, I wouldn't mind seeing the rest of the town."

"There's not much to see," said Al, "but the place does have a lot of character—a lot of history, too. My grandfather's, and even my father's, generations were tough generations—had to be—there weren't a lot of amenities back then."

"Was your father a miner?" asked Kelly.

"Yup. Grandfather, too. Most of the men at that time were in the mining industry to some degree. That's what drew them to Cripple Creek. There were a few that farmed the land, but not many."

"You probably know a lot about this town, Al. I find the name very unique. Do you know how it came to be known as Cripple Creek?"

"There's several versions, but I'll tell you the one most of the locals believe. It seems a farmer's cow was crossing the small stream that flowed through Poverty Gulch. The cow fell and broke its leg. Someone said, 'That's some Cripple Creek,' and I guess the name stuck."

Kelly smiled, and then took a bite of her cake. She held it on her tongue and slowly soaked in all the richness of the chocolate flavors.

"Oh, Ms. Hattie, this is deliciously decadent! I've never had a piece of devil's food cake this rich, this flavorful, this full of chocolate."

"Now you see, dear, why it is my favorite. I use several different types of chocolate, and lots of it. It was my mother's recipe. How she ever came up with it, I'll never know. It's not your typical devil's food, but I guess she called it that because of the white, fluffy icing."

As Kelly took another bite, she looked around the table at everyone, observing their differences. She thought them to be an interesting mix, but certainly not sinister. She told herself there had to be a logical explanation for the shadows at her door and for Tara's diary being placed facedown. She decided to put her concerns to rest and enjoy what time she had left at Ms. Hattie's.

Chapter Twenty-Two

It was shortly after noon when the snowplows made their way down to Hattie's place. Kelly watched for awhile as they struggled through the drifts. Kent had gone out to shovel the steps and walkway. Kelly at last had hope. She went upstairs to gather her few belongings. Having slept well for the first time since she arrived, she felt great. She knew once she got her car she would be free to come and go as she pleased. And she wouldn't feel confined if she did decide to stay at Hattie's. But she decided since she'd have to eat dinner elsewhere anyway, she would try Dolly's for a day or two.

She gathered her suitcase, coat, the scarf Ed loaned her and went to the parlor to wait. Robert and Al were playing a game of checkers but took notice when Kelly walked in with her suitcase.

"I guess you've decided to leave Cripple Creek," Robert said.

"Not really. I'm just moving downtown for a couple of days. Thought I'd take advantage of my time and explore for a day or two."

"I take it you're not continuing to Santa Fe?"

"No, I've lost interest. I'll linger here awhile, then head home."

"Gee, Robert, there goes our gourmet meals. Are you sure you have to leave, Kelly?" Al asked.

Kelly laughed. "You can't blame that on my leaving, Al. Once I get my car, I wouldn't be included in dinners anymore anyway."

"Kelly, I do hope you'll come back under more favorable conditions."

"Thank you, Robert. If I do return, I can assure you it will *not* be during a snowstorm."

The front door opened and Kent removed his boots and entered. "I haven't worked this hard in a long time," he said, as he removed his gloves and coat. "It's not perfect, but at least there's a path to the mailbox. And as far as the snowplows, one more sweep and I think they'll have the road passable." He didn't notice Kelly's suitcase until after he hung his coat up and was seated on the sofa.

He nodded towards the suitcase. "Does this mean you're ready to leave, Kelly?"

"I'm not leaving Cripple Creek right away, but since my car is at Dolly's, I thought I'd go up there for a night or two. I was looking for Ms. Hattie to tell her of my plans, but I haven't seen her since breakfast."

"Mother's in her room responding to several overdue letters that have piled up. I always tell her that if she'd get a computer, it would make life a lot easier. But she feels— especially with letters—that they need to be handwritten. She'll be out soon."

It never occurred to Kent how Kelly was going to get to Dolly's until Robert asked.

"The snow hasn't melted enough for you to get the car out of the garage, and I don't think you have enough daylight left to shovel that long driveway...even if Al and I help you. Will the snowmobile make it over the cleared streets?"

"Oh, no—I wouldn't expect you to do that," said Kelly. "Besides, I have a ride to Dolly's."

"You do?" said Kent and Robert in unison.

Oh dear, what will I say? she wondered. *I don't want to explain Joe to them. I can't even explain Joe to myself.*

"Yes. Someone from Dolly's said they would come down to get me when I'm ready. I just have to call once the road has been cleared." She noticed their questioning looks and realized she was being a little evasive, but she hoped they wouldn't pin her down. "When I saw the road was being plowed, I called Dolly's to see if they had a room for tonight," At least that part was true, and Joe was coming from Dolly's.

Kent got up and looked out the window. He stood there and watched the snowplow but said nothing. Kelly was sure, if given the opportunity, he would have talked more with her about Tara. She wondered if that was what he was thinking.

Robert and Al resumed their checker game. Kelly picked up a magazine from the coffee table.

"Do you think you'll ever get back this way, Kelly?" Kent asked, still focused on looking out the window.

"One never knows, but I doubt it will be during winter—although it has been quite an experience."

"I hope it hasn't been too unpleasant," he said, turning around.

"No, it hasn't. I didn't mean to give that impression. I'm very grateful for the hospitality I've received here. If I had to be captive, Ms. Hattie's was a nice place to be."

"I'm glad you feel that way. We do try to be hospitable."

Kelly was grateful for the friendliness that had been shown by everyone, but she was confused as to how she really felt about her stay at the bed-and-breakfast. She hoped being at Dolly's would give her the perspective she needed.

She looked at Robert and Al, then back at Kent. "I am very appreciative to all of you for making me feel welcome."

The checker game had been completed and both participants, along with Kent, gave their full attention.

"And I will tell you," she continued, "being confined does have its advantages. The moment it stopped snowing and the sun began to shine, I absorbed the beauty of winter in a whole new way—whereas before, I had taken it for granted. The scene out this picture window," she motioned towards where Kent stood, "was truly majestic."

Kent glanced out the window again and noticed the plows had left. "Kelly, I believe the road is as clear as it's going to be for awhile. Would you like me to call Dolly's for you?"

"Thank you, Kent, but that won't be necessary. I have the number right here in my purse. I'll call when I'm ready. I do want to say good-bye to Ms. Hattie before I leave."

"I'll go get Mother. I know she would want to say good-bye to you, too."

When he left the room, she reached in her purse and pulled out the piece of paper with Joe's cell number and dialed. Robert watched with interest. Al gathered the pieces to the checkerboard and put them away.

"Hello, Joe here."

"This is Kelly Murphy. I have a room there tonight and was told someone would come down to get me once the road had been cleared. I'm at Ms. Hattie's Bed & Breakfast, and the road has been cleared." She knew Robert had been watching. She felt awkward and hoped Joe wouldn't hang up on her.

"Kelly, is this you?"

"Yes, that's correct. Ten minutes would be perfect."

"Okay, sure, ten minutes, I'll be there. Should I wait in the car?"

She was relieved. He took the bait and played along.

"There's no need to get my bags, I only have one. I'll come out when I see you. Thanks, Good-bye." She hung up just as Hattie and Kent came into the room.

"So you've decided to leave us, Kelly."

Kelly stood and walked over to Hattie. "Yes, I think it best I leave before I wear out my welcome," she said with a smile.

"I doubt you would do that, dear, but I do understand. I'm sure you're anxious to get your car and the rest of your belongings."

"I can't thank you enough, Ms. Hattie, for all you've done. I especially appreciate the dinners you've prepared for me. I guess there is an advantage to being here during a blizzard. Had I not been detained, I might never have known what a blue ribbon devil's food cake tastes like."

"It was my pleasure. You'll have to come visit us again."

"I just may do that." She turned to Kent and shook his hand. He held it while she spoke. "And thank you, Kent. I will never forget that snowmobile ride," she said warmly.

Hattie stared at the clasped hands. Kent released his grip and Kelly pulled her hand free—but not before noticing the disturbed look on Hattie's face. She picked up her suitcase and looked out the window. Joe was out front, the car idling. After saying a friendly good-bye to Robert and Al, she opened the door and left.

Chapter Twenty-Three

They made small talk during the short drive back to Dolly's. Kelly looked out the window and assessed the piles of snow left by the snowplows. Joe waited patiently for an explanation of the strange conversation they'd had when she called him to let him know the roads had been cleared. Kelly was polite and appreciative for the ride, but she said nothing about the telephone call.

When they got to Dolly's, he pulled up next to her car and suggested she move it to the cleared parking lot in back. She was pleased to see that it was alright and that someone had shoveled around it.

"Kelly, follow me and I'll show you where to park."

She agreed and slowly drove around the block. The sky was clear, and since it was daylight, there was much to see that hadn't been visible when she'd first arrived in Cripple Creek during the blinding snowstorm. The buildings were old and interesting. Main Street didn't look over four or five blocks long and consisted mainly of one casino after another. It reminded her of a scene out of an old western movie, but instead of saloons, there were casinos.

She parked next to Joe. He grabbed the larger suitcase and she, the smaller one. They went into Dolly's through the back door. Once she was checked in, Joe helped carry her bags to the room.

"Why don't I give you about fifteen minutes to get settled, then meet me downstairs in the cafe?" he said, just as Kelly unlocked the door.

"Are you serious?" she asked, pushing the door open.

"You said you would have coffee with me." He set the suitcase on the bed. "Besides, I think you owe me an explanation."

Kelly knew he had to be confused by the phone call; she was confused, too, and wasn't sure how to explain her behavior. And she really didn't want to. She had hoped to brush it off.

Maybe I could tell him I'm a very private person and didn't want anyone at Hattie's to question me about letting someone I'd only met once come pick me up. That's why I pretended it was an employee from Dolly's. After all, that is why I acted that way—isn't it?

"Joe, I said I'd have coffee with you before I left town. Since I'm spending the night, it doesn't look as if I'll be leaving town right away."

"So, what's your point?" he said with a smirk on his face.

"The point being, we don't have to have coffee within the next fifteen minutes."

She could tell he wasn't ready to give up. *He's probably afraid if he gives me too much time to think about it, I'll censor what I say...and he'd be right.*

"Okay, then take thirty minutes. I'll go lose some more money while I wait." He left the room before she could utter a response.

Kelly watched him walk down the hall. She didn't know what to make of Joe Conrad. There was a part of him that frustrated her, even irritated her, and yet at the same time, she found his confidence and persistence appealing.

She had planned to wait an hour before going down to the cafe, but thirty minutes later, she was in the casino and headed in that direction. There was a Double Double Bonus poker machine by the cafe entrance where Joe was seated. Just as she walked up to him, four aces and a two popped up on the machine. Joe jumped up, clapped his hands, and shouted, "That's what I've been waiting for!"

"I know four aces are good, but just *how* good?"

"Darn good! I had the kicker—the two—so it pays top dollar for what I had in it. I've been playing quarters the whole time I've been here, but I decided to sit at the dollar machine so I could see you when you came down. I started off with one dollar, seemed to be holding my own, so I progressed to three dollars a hand—very unusual for me. You must have brought me luck, Kelly. I hit four aces with the kicker just as you walked up. I won $1,200!"

"That's great, Joe! As often as my friend, Tara, used to come, she never won this kind of money." Kelly didn't realize she had mentioned Tara's name until she noticed the raised eyebrows on Joe. She wondered if, by chance, he had run into her at Dolly's or at Ms. Hattie's when he was there. She didn't want to pursue it, so instead, continued to congratulate him on his winnings.

"Kelly, while I cash out, why don't you get us a table in the cafe?" She looked at him as though she wasn't sure she wanted to follow his command. "Please?" he added. "I'll be there shortly."

"Alright," she said. She watched him push the cash-out button, receive his payout ticket, and head to the cashier's cage. She looked over at the bar to see if Ed was there, but he wasn't. She wanted to return the borrowed scarf. She had also wanted to ask if he remembered Tara.

Kelly walked into the cafe and sat at a table in the back in an area less congested. A young man came over with a menu and a glass of water.

"There will be two of us" she said, "but I don't think we'll need menus. Just coffee, please."

"Go ahead and leave the menu," Joe said as he pulled out a chair, "and bring another menu with the second water. Thanks."

"I know how to order coffee. I don't need a menu."

"I'm sure you do. It's nice to see you still have that edge about you. And to think I thought we could have a pleasant conversation. Maybe I should go to my room and call you. You're easier to talk to on the phone—except when you're talking in code." He sounded gruff, but when he looked at her, he smiled.

Kelly felt she was seeing him for the very first time. She hadn't paid attention before as to how he looked. She liked what she saw. He wasn't handsome in the clean-cut boyish way that Kent was, but he had nice, strong, attractive features. She liked the gray around his temples. And she even liked the few sprigs of gray sprinkled throughout his full head of hair. She thought the mustache made him look even more masculine...she liked that too—along with his smile.

"I'm having déjà vu," began Kelly. "Once again I'm in the cafe and feeling like I need to apologize for my behavior. Usually I'm not like this. I really am a nice person. You must bring out my worst side," she teased.

"I've been known to have that effect on people," Joe smiled.

The waiter showed up with coffee, extra water, and menus. "We don't start serving dinner until five o'clock. But if you don't want to wait another thirty minutes, I can get you a sandwich."

"Coffee's fine for now. We won't be ready to eat for another hour or so, but check back on the coffee."

"Okay, I'll leave the menus and check back later."

Kelly sat there and said nothing, even though she wanted to. She wanted to tell him she could speak for herself. Half of her felt annoyed that he thought she'd have dinner with him; the other half was pleased that he wanted to have dinner with her.

"Hey, relax. You don't have to have dinner with me. I didn't need to explain to the waiter that I was hoping to talk you into it, however. Kelly, I just won $1,200! I want to celebrate! And I'm tired of talking to machines. You're a breath of fresh air. So I'll ask you properly: if

I don't anger you through coffee, will you have dinner with me?"

"Now that's a back-handed invitation, but I do like the loophole. Okay, if we survive coffee, I'll stay for dinner."

"That's a deal!" He reached over and shook her hand. Kelly liked the strength in his handshake. She wasn't good at guessing someone's age, but she thought he must be about ten years older than she. She sensed him to be secure with his own persona: he didn't seem the type to need approval, and she doubted he ever gave a compliment he didn't mean.

"What's first on the agenda?" she asked.

"At the risk of getting off on the wrong foot, I'd like for you to explain the strange phone call."

She sighed, then began. "Joe, I'm a private person. I don't like everyone knowing my business. I didn't know how to explain that a perfect stranger was coming to pick me up. That's all there was to it. And by the way, I do appreciate you playing along."

"You don't strike me as the type who worries about what others think."

"You may be right. Let's just say, I wasn't comfortable explaining *you*."

The waiter came back. Kelly picked up her menu, relieved for the interruption, and even though she wasn't hungry yet, proceeded to order. She knew this conversation wasn't over, but she hoped to stall it until after dinner.

Chapter Twenty-Four

The parlor was quiet. Hattie had made herself a cup of tea and sipped on it as the wood-burning stove was dying down for the night. Business had been slow that winter, and the storm didn't help matters. And as much as she needed the business, she was glad Kelly was gone. There was something about her that was troubling, and Hattie was disturbed that she hadn't left town. She was concerned that Kent might become interested in her. There was also something else that bothered her: she wondered why Kelly had decided to stay longer— and at Dolly's. There was nothing in Cripple Creek for Kelly so why hadn't she continued on to Santa Fe? Did it have anything to do with Tara?

"Mother, you're up a bit late, aren't you?" Kent asked. He went to the stove to shake down the remains.

"I suppose I am."

"Usually when you're up late, it's because you're concerned about business. I have some news that might cheer you up. Do you remember the Collins'? They were here last year at this time."

"I'm not sure that I do."

"Middle-aged fun couple from Denver. He was the one who was always telling jokes at breakfast."

"Yes, yes, I remember now. What about them?"

"Mr. Collins called me on my cell phone. He didn't realize he hadn't called the main line. They booked for next weekend. They also have another couple coming with them. We have two rooms booked! Business is looking up."

"I am very glad to hear that, Kent." She watched him a moment as he finished putting the stove to sleep for the night. She was proud of him and always felt he was a good son. "Kent, you seemed to have spent some time with Kelly while she was here. Did she talk with you about her friend, Tara?"

"I spent very little time with Kelly, Mother. Why would you be interested in what she might have said about Tara? Is it your morbid sense of curiosity?" he asked, in a sharper tone than what he had intended.

"There's no reason to be nasty, Kent."

"Mother, be honest. You never liked Tara. Why should you care if anything was said? It shouldn't make any difference to you whether Kelly talked to me about Tara or not."

Hattie looked wounded. "Just because I had some issues with her doesn't mean I didn't like her. She had many endearing qualities."

"Stop the pretense, Mother. It's easy to like her now—she's dead! She can't be a threat to you any longer." Kent's voice cracked and tears formed in his eyes. He couldn't say anymore, so he left the room.

Hattie sat there with her mouth open. She wanted to speak but couldn't. She felt hurt to think he had talked to her that way, that he thought those things of her. And for the first time, she felt his hurt over Tara.

She wasn't right for you, Kent. You didn't listen to me about Mary and look how that turned out. I can't stand to see you hurt. I don't ever want another woman to hurt you the way Mary did. You'll understand one day. You will. You'll see. I didn't wish any harm to Tara. But Kent, you were moving too fast.

Chapter Twenty-Five

Kelly was relieved Joe hadn't pressed her for more of an explanation. Dinner was pleasant. They made small talk, mostly about the charm of Cripple Creek. She found him easy to talk to. She decided to trust her instincts and tell him more.

"I really can't explain the phone call. I don't understand it myself. Ms. Hattie's B & B wasn't what I had anticipated. And I don't know how to explain that either. Everyone was very nice, but it was just *different*." She could tell she had Joe's interest.

"How do you mean, different?"

She wanted to tell Joe about everything: the footsteps at her door, Tara's diary being touched, and her doubts about Ms. Hattie. She needed to tell someone, but she wondered if he'd laugh at her or think she was paranoid. She finally decided that he was, at least, someone to talk to. And if he thought she was crazy—so what? She'd probably never see him again anyway.

"Before I continue, I'd like to ask you a question. You said you had stayed at Ms. Hattie's once. What did you think of your experience?"

"Kelly, when I stayed there, the place was full. I met Hattie's two boarders, along with the other guests, but I couldn't tell you their names. I wish I had paid more attention. Everyone was friendly and nice, but I didn't notice anything out of the ordinary. It was a long time ago. Maybe I'd feel differently now. I told you, I'm not a bed-and-breakfast type person. Maybe you aren't, either. Have you ever stayed at one before?"

"No. And you could be right. Maybe I read more into something than what was really there. It comes with the territory."

"What do you mean it comes with the territory?" Joe asked.

"I'm a reporter for the *Sentinel* newspaper. I have a wonderful editor, who is also a good friend, and he has always taught me to look beneath the surface. I cover a lot of special assignments for the paper, and I'm used to digging, but now I'm feeling silly, and I'm sure it can all be reasoned out."

"You're a reporter—how interesting. I don't know how much help I can be, but I would like to hear about your experience at the B & B. If nothing else, talking about it might help to put it in perspective."

"I hope you're right," she said, and proceeded to describe her stay at Ms. Hattie's. She felt comfortable with Joe. He seemed honest and trustworthy. And she wasn't concerned that what she said would be discussed elsewhere. She even told him about Tara and her diary, but she didn't tell him she was suspicious as to how Tara died.

Joe listened intently. When she finished, he shook his head. "Kelly, I don't know if any of it means anything, but I can understand why you felt uncomfortable. Let me play devil's advocate for awhile. I'll address the footsteps first. Since Al has a room upstairs, it seems reasonable that he might have been the one who paused at your door. Maybe he went to the bathroom half asleep and paused for a moment, thinking it was his room. Then realized it wasn't, and left."

"That did cross my mind to begin with, but Ms. Hattie told me Al had a toilet and sink in his room. He only uses the hall bathroom to shower. Joe, I distinctly heard someone on the stairs. The steps are old, and they creak. I don't think it was Al. That's why it doesn't make sense. Why would someone come up the stairs at four in the morning and stand in front of my door? There weren't any other guests at Ms. Hattie's that night."

"It's strange, Kelly. I wish I had an answer, but I don't. As far as your friend's diary being touched—you even said yourself that you were very sick that night. Couldn't it be a simple case of being preoccupied and just not paying attention to how you placed the diary? I'm sure if I was thinking about grabbing the wastebasket, I wouldn't have thought about proper placement of a book."

Kelly tried to remember all the details of that night, especially why she had felt so strongly that the diary had been touched. "Joe, I thought about that, too, but there are some things I'm very precise about. And to the best of my recollection, I had put the diary down before I got to the point of needing the wastebasket." She wanted to tell him she felt Tara's presence that night, and about the strong urge she had had to turn away from the wall and towards the diary. But she didn't dare tell him that. She was concerned if she did, he'd have thought her to be a flake for sure.

"You said you left your door open when you rushed to the bathroom. If someone had walked in looking for you, what reason would they have had to pick up the diary?"

"I know it sounds crazy, Joe, but I really sensed that someone had." She was beginning to wish she had never mentioned any of it.

"Kelly, you said your friend, Tara, visited Ms. Hattie's quite often. Was there any reason she preferred staying there rather than at one of the casinos?"

"She liked Ms. Hattie a lot—at least in the beginning. But I believe the main reason she kept returning was because of Kent, Ms. Hattie's son. She and Kent became very good friends. I even thought for awhile, Tara was falling in love with him, but then their relationship seemed to take a turn. They still remained friends, but in the months before Tara's death, I don't remember her mentioning Kent.

"The other day, Kent told me he had been very fond of Tara. He said they used to do special things together and would meet at different places. I always had the feeling Tara cared a lot more for Kent than she wanted to let on. It's funny, but after Tara told me she and Kent were just friends, she didn't really talk about him anymore…and I didn't ask. At that time, the newspaper was short staffed, and I was working a lot of overtime. I think about it now and regret not taking the time to talk to her about him. I wish I knew why it ended."

"If you're reading Tara's diary, Kelly, doesn't she write about Kent?"

"Yes, she does. How much, I'm not sure. I've just gotten to the part when she first meets him." She took a deep breath. She had said far more than she had planned. "I think I went beyond explaining my phone behavior. And since neither one of us can come up with any conclusive reasons for the strange happenings at Ms. Hattie's, I think I have talked enough. Now it's your turn, Joe. Tell me a little about yourself."

Chapter Twenty-Six

Kelly and Joe talked all through dinner, dessert, and coffee with Baileys. She learned that he was once on the police force, but he didn't tell her he worked in the homicide division. He also didn't tell her he had gone private. He only mentioned he was burned out and had moved on to other things. Then he changed the subject and talked about his winnings. They joked about whether he'd still be ahead when he left town.

By the time Kelly got back to her room, it was half past nine. She was tired but wasn't ready for bed. She looked at the suitcases and realized she wouldn't be leaving in a day or two. She didn't know why, but she had a need to finish Tara's diary in Cripple Creek. Maybe it was nothing more than having regrets for not coming here when Tara had invited her.

She read for two hours before she came across something that might have explained why Tara had stopped talking about Ms. Hattie and Kent. There were pages of day-to-day life—hiking, work, and her visits to Cripple Creek, which had become more frequent than every other month. Her feelings for Kent had definitely grown. Ms. Hattie had always seemed pleased to see her until

Kent went to visit Tara and they hiked the Monument. The next time she went to Cripple Creek, Hattie was cool. Tara wrote about being confused by the change she saw in her, but it was what she wrote next that disturbed Kelly.

Nov. 10th. _Hi, Friend—I just got back from Cripple Creek and felt the need to write. I've done nothing but think all the way home. Maybe if I write my feelings down, I can make sense of this weekend._

It's been five weeks since Kent and I hiked the Monument together. Something very special happened between us that weekend. I felt Kent might be falling in love with me, and I knew I was in love with him. Since that visit, we've talked on the phone almost every day. I was so excited to see him this weekend! He surprised me Saturday night and took me to the Broadmoor Hotel in Colorado Springs for dinner. It was one of the most wonderful evenings I think I have ever had. The place is beautiful—and expensive. I felt so special! The night was perfect. I wouldn't have thought anything could have spoiled it.

It was very late before we got back—we had an after-dinner drink and lingered for awhile. Neither one of us were anxious to go back to the B & B. We talked for hours. Kent told me about his failed marriage to Mary and I shared things with him that only Kelly knew about. I felt close to him, and everything felt right.

Almost midnight, in fact, when we pulled into the driveway. We hesitated, not wanting to get out of the car, not wanting the evening to end. Once inside, we could tell everyone was *asleep—it was very quiet. Kent invited me to his room for a nightcap. I accepted. Then he asked me to stay the night—and I did. It wasn't planned, it just happened—but it felt so right. I chuckled to myself because we both had talked about wanting to take things slow and just enjoy the friendship we were building.*

The night was magical. I woke the next morning in Kent's arms, and I didn't want to leave. It seemed like a dream, but the best dream I'd ever had. I remember thinking; oh please, don't let this end!

I guess we slept in, because Ms. Hattie knocked on Kent's door and told him he needed to get the fire going in the wood-burning stove. He told her he'd be there in a minute and jumped out of bed. What happened next was strange. While Kent was putting his clothes on, I headed for the shower. He stopped me and suggested I shower upstairs in the guest bathroom. He wanted me to wait to leave his room until he was sure his mother was in the kitchen so she wouldn't see me. I admit, it would have been uncomfortable to run into her, but it surprised me that Kent was concerned. I told myself he was just looking out for me and not wanting me to feel awkward. I agreed to wait in his room. He checked to see if the coast was clear. When he gave me the okay, I left.

There I was, starting up the stairs on the way to my room, my hair not combed and wearing the same clothes I had on the night before. Out of nowhere, I hear Ms. Hattie say good morning. When I turned to reply, she looked at me—I mean really looked at me. I knew I looked a mess, but the expression on her face was almost threatening. You would have thought I had slapped her. Without saying another word, she turned and walked away. I can understand her displeasure in seeing me that way. I can even understand her disappointment in Kent and me, but I thought she liked me, and I wasn't prepared for the way she was treating me. I might as well have worn a scarlet letter across my chest for all to see that I had sinned.

By the time I had freshened up and gone down to breakfast, there were two other guests already seated, joining Robert and Al. They must have checked in after Kent and I left for dinner the night before. I said good morning to all. The guests were friendly and exchanged greetings. Robert and Al were more cordial than usual. I wondered if Ms. Hattie had said anything to them.

She served the other guests first, then Robert and Al. I was served last. She didn't speak to anyone, just went about her business. I was hoping to see Kent, but I didn't.

Once everyone was through with breakfast, the dining room cleared out—except for me. I stayed in hopes of talking to Ms. Hattie. I wanted to explain to her just how much I cared about her son, and that it wasn't a one-night stand. She never returned to the dining room. I was to check out by eleven o'clock so I went upstairs to pack.

As I was packing, there was a knock on my door. I opened it and Kent stood there with the most beautiful smile on his face. "Hi, gorgeous," he said, pulling me towards him. He kissed away the unpleasant morning. Maybe I should have told him about the episode with his mother, but I didn't. I didn't want that to be the last thing we discussed before I left. I wanted to remember his arms around me. He gently kissed my forehead, then each cheek before pressing his lips to mine for one more lingering, passionate, so-long-for-now kiss. My knees felt *weak. I thought if he moved I would melt to the floor. It was the perfect finish to our fabulous weekend...or so I thought.*

In the back of my mind, I could hear someone coming up the stairs, and yet strangely, it wasn't registering. It must not have registered with Kent, either, because he also didn't move. It wasn't until Ms. Hattie cleared her throat in an exaggerated manner that we pulled away. Her face was flushed. I could tell she was making a conscious effort to maintain her cool. She suggested to Kent that he take my suitcase to the car. He picked it up and said he'd meet me outside.

Ms. Hattie glared at me but didn't say a word. I tried to talk to her. I told her I had very special feelings for her son and felt blessed that he seemed to reciprocate those feelings. I said we may not have handled the weekend properly, but I hoped she would understand. And I, like her, only wanted the best for Kent.

As I'm writing this, and remembering what she said to me, I am visibly shaking. She walked over to me and got within six inches of my face. She said, and I quote...

"You little hussy! How dare you tell me you want what's best for my son! As if you would know what's best for him. I know all about you. I had you checked out. I know you can't keep a relationship. I also know you have two male friends you sleaze around with. I'm telling you—stay away from my son. And if you don't, you'll wish you had."

I could hardly speak; my heart was in my throat. I tried to explain Jack and Pete to her. I tried to tell her they were just friends, and I only went out with them because I wasn't ready for a relationship. I told her I hadn't seriously been interested in anyone for a very long time—until Kent came along. And now that I found someone I really cared about, did she seriously think I could just turn my back and walk out of his life? Didn't she realize how much that would hurt him?

Kent opened the front door and called up the stairs. Hattie told him she was saying good-bye and I'd be right down. I thought for a moment that she was considering what I'd said. Maybe she could see my sincerity, my concern, and my feelings for Kent. She backed away from me, then said in a stern, but less threatening, tone, "Tara, think long and hard about what I've said. And if you care about Kent, you have to realize a long-distance relationship is not in his best interest. You are never to tell him we had this conversation. That way, you can leave with your reputation intact. Believe me, Tara, I can be very convincing. Kent has known me far longer than he's known you. I'm the one who will be with him every day. He needs this business as much as I do. So, Tara, this is what I want you to do: Back off, but I want you to back off gradually. When he calls, tell him you're not ready for a relationship. Tell him you only want to be friends. Then, don't come back."

I walked past her and said nothing. My heart was too heavy. When I got downstairs, I tried to act nonchalant, but Kent sensed the difference. We walked to the car and he asked if something was wrong. I told him I was just feeling a little overwhelmed by our whirlwind weekend. He seemed okay with it and said he'd call me tomorrow.

I'm feeling numb. I can't make sense out of any of it. I don't know if I can just walk away. But I know how committed he is to helping his mother run the B & B. How can I come between that? Maybe tomorrow will shed new light...maybe I imagined it all...

Kelly closed the diary and tried to process what she had read. She knew there had been a couple of months, due to her work schedule, when she and Tara had not kept in touch. Could all this have happened during that time? She wondered if Tara would have told her about that last visit at Ms. Hattie's had she not been so wrapped up in work. But knowing Tara as she did, she also knew there were times she wouldn't talk about a painful situation until she had worked through it.

It was after midnight and she didn't want to read anymore. She felt sad. She hurt for Tara. And she cried for her.

Chapter Twenty-Seven

Al put the checkerboard away, yawned, and told Robert he was calling it a night. It was late. Their game had started later than usual. Al's favorite team was playing Monday night football, and he didn't want to play checkers until it was over. After Al left, Robert lingered, even though the ambers had cooled in the stove.

"I heard Al going up the stairs. I was hoping you'd still be here, Robert."

"You seem restless, Hattie. Is there a problem?"

She sat down, folded her hands, and looked at him. "We've been friends for a long time, but it has been a strange friendship, don't you think?"

"I'm not sure I understand what you're trying to say."

"I've been doing a lot of thinking tonight. Robert, since Larry's death, you have genuinely always been here for me. You're concerned when I'm troubled. When there's a problem, you ask me how I am. Whenever I need help, you're there. And when I need to talk, you listen. Most importantly, you care enough to disagree with me. Although I must admit, I don't readily appreciate it sometimes."

He wasn't sure where she was going with this conversation. He reached over, patted her hand, and smiled. "I believe you accurately described the definition of a friend. We *are* friends, Hattie, there's nothing unusual—or commendable—about my behavior."

"Other than idle chitchat, when have I ever asked how *you* were doing? Or what your interests are, or why you've stayed here all these years? I know very little about you, Robert. And I know nothing to speak of about your family. I have limited knowledge of your background, and I'm not really sure—since you no longer work in the mines—why you still stay in Cripple Creek."

He felt uneasy. What brought this about? He wondered if she had decided to close the bed-and-breakfast. Was she going to ask him to leave? That was something he couldn't even fathom. He would have liked to have told her that he's stayed because he has been in love with her for years. But he feared if he ever said as much, she would surely ask him to leave. Hattie had made it clear on several occasions, ever since Larry's death, that she had no interest in the affection of the opposite sex. And he knew she especially felt that way once Kent moved back home. Robert convinced himself he would be satisfied with her friendship, but deep down he had always longed for more.

"Hattie, you said you were doing some thinking. Is there a point to all this?" he asked hesitantly.

She took a moment before she answered, which made Robert even more nervous. "I realize I haven't been much of a friend. How can I be a friend and know so little about you? Maybe I don't know how to be a friend. I never thought of myself as selfish, but I can see that I am."

He was relieved. She wasn't going to ask him to leave. "I think you're being too harsh on yourself. I can honestly say that I've never thought of you as a selfish person. A bit stubborn perhaps..."

Hattie raised an eyebrow.

"...Oh, admit it," he continued. "However, I will say, it serves you well. Your tenacity always tends to get things accomplished."

"Robert, be honest with me. What do you see as my weakness, my biggest liability?"

"I don't know if I'd call it a weakness, but I do see it as a liability." He watched her expression change. He knew she didn't want to hear the rest of his thoughts. "Hattie, I say this because you are my friend. You need to quit interfering in Kent's life. I see Kent getting more agitated with you and even resentful. I'm fearful there will come a day when he'll give up his interest in the bed-and-breakfast and walk out the door forever."

"Your words are strong, Robert."

"Yes, they are, but they're true."

"Kent knows I've devoted my life to him. He might get irritated at times, but it passes. He would never walk out of my life; he knows what that would do to me."

Robert also knew what it would do to her. If Kent met someone, fell in love, and moved away, Hattie would be devastated. It would be worse than losing Larry in that horrible accident. But he also felt if Kent hadn't moved back, maybe she would have been open to more than a one-sided friendship.

"As I told you, I've been doing a lot of thinking tonight," Hattie continued. "Maybe I have been too possessive of Kent. I've thought about these past years since he moved back home. I felt the hurt and pain Mary caused him, and I guess I was blinded by that. Perhaps at times I have been overly protective. But I can honestly say, on a couple of occasions, I was right in how I felt. And I know one day, he'll thank me. When the right person comes into his life, he will appreciate my feelings," she concluded.

"Hattie, we all, as human beings—as adults, have to be allowed to make our own mistakes. But am I hearing you correctly? Are you saying you realize now that you've been too involved in Kent's life and you're ready to back off?"

"I'm saying I'm ready to be more open-minded. I will continue to influence when I feel the need, but I'm willing to be less smothering. I want Kent to be happy. I thought the business was enough for him, but I see it isn't."

Robert had always wished Hattie would focus less on Kent, but he had come to accept that his own interests in her had limitations. He derived pleasure in seeing her content and would do most anything for her. He had even spoken to Kent on occasion about the negative traits he observed in someone Kent might have seemed interested in—not because he believed there to be such traits, but after much urging from Hattie, she finally convinced him to do so. He delighted in her pleasure and felt it was worth compromising his own beliefs. He thought it a small price to pay to gain her favor.

"Relationships are important," said Robert. "Most men cannot exist without them. Sometimes work alone isn't enough."

"I understand that, and I'm willing to accept it. However, there is one situation I will discourage from happening, then I'll back off."

He hesitated to ask. He wasn't sure he wanted to know. He had an inkling of her concern but hoped he was wrong. He waited. When he didn't respond, she continued.

"Don't you think it strange that Kelly hasn't left town?"

"To be honest, I've not given it any thought."

"I tell you, Robert, there's something very uncomfortable about that girl. She didn't want to be in Cripple Creek, so why is she staying? The phone call she got the other day was from someone right here in Cripple Creek. He wanted to meet her for coffee. If this is the first time she's been in town, who does she know who would want to have coffee with her?"

"How do you know what was said on Kelly's phone call? Did she tell you about it, or did you eavesdrop?"

"Of course she didn't tell me about her phone call. I didn't eavesdrop, per se; I just happened to be in the dining room and overheard part of the conversation. Never mind about that. There is more that I find curious. When Kelly told us about Tara Medcalf, she said she thought

Tara had stayed here a day or two. If they were friends, she would have known Tara visited often. And she would have known about Kent."

"There you go again, Hattie, reading more into something than what is there. Friendship has many levels. Perhaps Kelly and Tara were casual friends and didn't discuss their personal lives. Besides, why should it concern you? I didn't get the impression Kelly had any interest in Kent."

"Did you see the way Kelly looked when she talked about Tara? I could tell they were closer than casual friends."

"Say they *were* closer, what does it have to do with Kent?"

She didn't answer right away. Robert watched her; he could tell she had something specific on her mind. She got up and walked to the darkened window. She stood there a moment before she spoke.

"Remember the girl Kent was involved with several years ago?"

"How could I forget?"

"You couldn't understand why I was so upset about that relationship."

"No, I couldn't—other than it was his first serious relationship since Mary."

"The woman was divorced and just starting a new career. She didn't have any money. But she knew Kent did."

Robert looked puzzled. To his knowledge, Kent was of average means—no more.

"There's no reason for you to know this, but I'm going to tell you anyway. And when I do, maybe you'll understand my concerns for Kent a little better.

"I knew Larry had a life insurance policy. A few weeks after the accident, I called the insurance company to file a claim. It wasn't a priority at the time of his death, and I had enough to cover the funeral. I never read over the policy. I didn't realize it had a double indemnity clause in it for accidental death. It was a lot of money. I set up a trust for Kent. I didn't tell him about it until after his divorce. Then I turned the trust over to him. He has a substantial monthly income from the trust fund. Unfortunately, he made the mistake of telling that girl—I cannot think of her name—about the trust. I felt she was more interested in the money than in Kent. That's why, Robert, I wanted your help in breaking up the relationship. You see, it wasn't only because I thought he'd gotten involved too soon after his divorce. Since then, I've encouraged Kent not to discuss his money with anyone."

He took a moment to absorb what he had just been told. He realized there was still a lot about Hattie that he didn't know. "Even if your feelings were correct, and the relationship was all about the money, what does this have to do with Kelly?"

"What do we know about Kelly? If the only reason she's in Cripple Creek is because of a temporary detour due to the blizzard, wouldn't you think she would have left town as soon as she could? No, Robert, I don't think Kelly's here by accident. I think Kent told Tara about the money. And if he did, I'm sure Tara told Kelly."

"Hattie, don't do this to yourself. Don't speculate and don't give your thoughts fuel. Go back to the beginning of our conversation, the part where you said you were going to back off."

"I meant what I said and I will, but not before Kelly leaves town. She makes me uneasy. I won't rest until she's gone."

Chapter Twenty-Eight

Joe was up early. For the first time in several nights, he had slept well. He thought about Kelly, and about their conversation concerning her stay at Ms. Hattie's. He liked Kelly, but he didn't have her figured out yet. He replayed the evening over and over again, and he wasn't sure he bought her story as to why she had decided to stay in Cripple Creek. He learned a long time ago to trust his gut feeling—it had always served him well when he was on the police force. He had often wondered if he was born with a good sense of judgment or if he developed it when he was in law enforcement. All he knew was when he paid attention to his *feelings*, they seldom proved him wrong. And he was having a gut feeling about Kelly. He may not have her figured out, but he believed she was honest. And he felt he could trust her.

When he first met Kelly, she was annoyed that the blizzard had detained her. She was anxious to leave Cripple Creek and be on her way. He knew from her conversation last night that she was uncomfortable staying at Ms. Hattie's. And if she didn't like to gamble, then what was her reason for staying? He thought about her friend, Tara, and Tara's relationship to Kent. He wondered if Kelly had read something in the diary that changed her mind about leaving. Or could it be possible that Kelly herself didn't fully understand why she had decided to stay?

Kelly's a reporter, she's curious by nature, he thought. *She's been reading her friend's diary, and she knows Tara was fond of Cripple Creek. It's probably nothing more than missing her friend and wanting to experience a place that was meaningful to her.* Joe didn't know what to believe, but he didn't have any better thoughts at the moment.

He had wanted to call Kelly and see if she'd have breakfast with him, but he felt it was still too early. He decided to kill time by going through Tiffany Buckley's file—then he'd call Kelly.

He opened the file and decided to focus on Tiffany's visits to Cripple Creek. He didn't have a lot of information about them, and what he did have was sketchy at best. She lived in Colorado Springs, she worked in Colorado Springs, and she died in Colorado Springs. He couldn't find the connection between Cripple Creek and her death, but still it haunted him. The last weekend of her life had been spent here. She checked out Sunday morning and returned to Colorado Springs for her afternoon appointment with someone who called himself Jason Goldbloom. He scratched his head. Something kept nagging at him about that weekend. It didn't make sense that Tiffany would have gone to Cripple Creek the same weekend she had an appointment to show a million dollar home. He knew she had time to get back home for the appointment, but it still didn't make sense. She was divorced, hadn't been with the real estate company very long, and she needed the money.

Joe didn't know Tiffany that well, but he knew her parents. From what they had told him, to their knowledge, Tiffany wasn't much of a gambler. She enjoyed going with friends and always had a good time. But going to Cripple Creek wasn't something she would normally do by herself, and yet, she did go by herself. But her mom was quick to add that Tiffany didn't talk much to her parents about her personal life.

Joe paced back and forth, trying to figure out what he was missing. *She went on a weekend trip when she should have been home preparing for an appointment that could have financially made a tremendous difference in her life. Why would Tiffany have chosen that weekend to go to Cripple Creek? Why? Unless...*

"That's it! That's got to be it!" he yelled aloud. *Tiffany must have been seeing someone here. She had probably made plans to see him that weekend before she ever set up the appointment with the so-called Jason Goldbloom. If I can find out who Tiffany was seeing, maybe then I can shed some light on who might have used Jason Goldbloom's identity to set up the appointment with her.*

It wasn't going to be easy. It had been five years since Tiffany's death. But there was something Kelly had said last night that triggered his thoughts. He picked up the phone and hoped she would meet him for breakfast.

Chapter Twenty-Nine

Kelly sipped her coffee as she studied Joe. She questioned why he had asked her to have breakfast with him. He'd said very little but appeared to have a lot on his mind. His attention seemed focused on Carla. He commented on her work schedule. It seemed that since the blizzard, there was no rhyme or reason as to whether she'd be working the morning or evening shift. Kelly was fascinated by his interest in Carla.

Carla reminded Kelly of a marine drill sergeant. She was a large-framed woman but not fat, more on the solid side. She wore very little makeup, and her hair was bobbed short. Although she was usually pleasant, most of the time she had an edge about her. Kelly had the impression Carla wasn't someone you'd want to cross. She continued to watch Joe, but she couldn't be quiet any longer.

"What is it about Carla that intrigues you?"

It wasn't until she spoke that Joe realized he had been preoccupied. "I'm not sure. I can't figure her out and it bugs me. You're the journalist, what do you make of her?"

"Sorry to disappoint you, but I haven't given Carla much thought. Joe, is this the reason you asked me to breakfast, to help you sort out Carla?"

"No, of course not. But there is something I want to talk to you about." He paused when he saw Carla coming towards their table. "Although I'm not sure I want to discuss it here."

"Anything else for you this morning?"she asked abruptly.

"Not for me. How about you, Kelly?"

"No, I'm good, thank you."

"You guys want your check? Or do you want to hang around and gab awhile?"

"Does it matter if we linger?" Joe asked.

"Nah—not to me anyway. I'll leave your check now, that way I won't have to come back and bother you. Just whistle if you need anything." She put the check on the table and left.

"What's on your mind?" Kelly asked after Carla got out of hearing range.

"Kelly, I'm working on a cold case, and there may be a connection to Cripple Creek."

"Cold case?" she interrupted. "I thought you said you had left the police department."

"I did. I guess I'd better back up and start from the beginning..." Joe proceeded to fill her in on his background.

Kelly listened intently. She was intrigued to learn that he had once been a detective with the homicide division and had now gone private. He had just started telling her about Tiffany Buckley when her phone rang. She saw it was Stan.

"Excuse me, Joe. I'm sorry to interrupt you, but this is my editor—it might be important. Do you mind?"

"No, go right ahead."

As Kelly talked to Stan, she noticed Carla was attending to the table directly next to her. She lowered her voice.

"Stan, did they say they reviewed everything...including the autopsy report?"

"Yes. But here's the encouraging part, Kelly. Even though there isn't anything significant to raise a red flag, my buddy, Max Taylor over in homicide, said he had been skeptical from the start, but he had nothing to go on."

Kelly felt a tremendous sense of relief and, at the same time, a rush of adrenalin. To think, finally, someone may be on the same page. "Did you tell Max how well Tara knew the terrain, and how unlikely it would have been for her to accidently fall?"

"Max and I spent a lot of time going over several different scenarios, none of which made any sense, especially given Tara's familiarity of the area. Kelly, I have something else to tell you, but you have to promise not to get your hopes up. I was going to wait until you got back to tell you, but I know what it will mean to you." He paused for only a second, but it seemed like an eternity to her.

"Tell me what, Stan? I'm not making any promises," she said in anticipation. Her voice raised a notch; not only did she have Joe's attention, but Carla still remained at the table nearby.

"Kelly, Max said he would reopen the case as unsolved. He wants to meet with you when you get back."

With all the emotion that had been restrained for months, she let out a sigh so deep her voice seemed to have left with it. She managed to tell Stan she would head home the next day.

"Don't leave yet. Max can't meet with you until next week. Stay where you are a few more days. You need this time alone."

"We'll see, Stan, we'll see. I'll call you tomorrow with my plans."

"Okay, just remember, this is only the haystack. We still have to find the needle."

"I know. Stan, I cannot thank you enough. I know you had a lot to do with influencing Max's decision."

"Well, kiddo, you were pretty persuasive. It wasn't my thoughts that influenced Max. I was just the conveyor. Take care and don't hurry home. Good-bye."

She said good-bye and placed the phone back in her purse. She could only imagine what Joe must have thought. She knew he had heard every word of her end of the conversation.

"Come on, Kelly, let's get out of here. You look like you could use a drink."

"I probably could, but it *is* still morning."

Since Carla was no longer in sight, Joe left cash on the table for their breakfast. Once in the casino, he suggested they go to his room so they could talk in private. Kelly raised an eyebrow in doubt.

"I have a small sitting area with a sofa," he said, "and I'm sure the maid has cleaned the room by now. She usually comes early. I also have a bottle of brandy in my room. If you feel threatened, you can scream. This place is old, and I'm sure someone will hear you," he teased.

"I'm learning more about you all the time, Mr. Conrad, and one thing I've come to believe is that you are trustworthy. And I agree, it will be better to talk in private. I might even take you up on that brandy. Right now I'm feeling like I could use some."

"Ah...I can see I have you in the palm of my hand," he said with a wink, trying to lighten her spirits.

"That will be the day," she responded quickly, then smiled and followed him to his room.

Chapter Thirty

Joe listened carefully as Kelly shared her suspicions concerning the cause of Tara's death. She paused, slowly sipped the brandy, then continued. She told him—word for word—of her conversation with Stan. He was silent. Many thoughts went through his mind. He wondered if there could have been a connection between Tara's death and Tiffany's, but realistically, he knew that wasn't likely. Neither Tara nor Tiffany died in Cripple Creek, but both deaths were made to look like an accident. He was caught up with what Kelly was saying and had forgotten for the moment why he had asked her to breakfast.

Once Kelly put the brandy glass down and gestured she wanted no more, Joe was ready to discuss his unanswered questions pertaining to Tiffany. He hoped Kelly's input might shed some new light, especially if she approached the information from a different angle than what he had been exploring. And he hoped she could help to explain the gnawing gut feeling he had every time he visited Cripple Creek. Considering her conversation with Stan, he knew he'd better take things slowly. He certainly didn't want to appear insensitive. She was a reporter and used to dealing with facts, but Tara was her best friend...and her death was still raw.

"I can appreciate what Stan's phone call must have meant to you," he began. "It's not easy trying to validate your feelings when no one else is buying into them. I'm glad Max is willing to hear you out. Most importantly, Max has also questioned whether or not Tara's death was accidental. You get a guy like that on your side—especially when he believes there's some substance in what you're telling him—and he won't give up." He watched her take a deep breath. Even after the brandy, she still looked like a wounded animal that had been rescued but wasn't sure it was going to be alright. "Kelly, you okay?"

"I think so. It's strange, Joe, but I'm not sure what I'm feeling right now. Part of me feels angry because three months have passed, and what clues there might have been may be lost. And I feel regret that I didn't pursue the uneasy feelings I had sooner and with more tenacity. But above all, there's this conflicting feeling of sadness and hope: sadness for feeling I've let Tara down, and a sense of hopefulness that we can finally find out what really happened to her and bring her the justice she deserves."

"Kelly, I can understand the flood of emotion, but listen to me. You even said yourself that there was no evidence to support anything other than it being an accident. Because of you, all the questions you've had pertaining to her death may finally be answered. If you ask me, I think Tara's one lucky gal to have a friend like you."

"I hope so, Joe." She took a deep breath and smiled. It was obvious by the look on her face that there was a renewed sense of purpose. She changed the subject.

"Hey, you asked me to breakfast to discuss a cold case you're working on. You had just started telling me about Tiffany when Stan called. You said you felt there was a connection to Cripple Creek, but didn't you say she died in Colorado Springs?"

"Yes. Let me finish filling you in on the Tiffany Buckley case. Then I have a few questions I'd like to go over with you. I think it will soon become clear in what direction I'm heading."

Joe talked for a long time. He meticulously went over every detail, first from Tiffany's death appearing to be an accident to Jason Goldbloom and, finally, to his gut feeling that the answer to solving Tiffany's murder lay in Cripple Creek.

"Joe, I think you're onto something. This is going to sound strange, and I probably shouldn't tell you. But when you mentioned your gut feeling about the connection to Cripple Creek, I had the weirdest sensation go through my entire body—almost like an affirmation screaming in my head—'yes!' Believe me, I'm not psychic, but my instincts, on more than one occasion, have proven to be correct."

"I have no doubt, and that's why I wanted to talk to you. Kelly, you have a sharp mind, and I'm hoping by reviewing the case with you, I'll find the missing link. This, by the way, brings me to the first item I wanted to ask you about. You mentioned at dinner that Tara had been seeing Ms. Hattie's son, Kent. Do you know how they met?"

"Yes. Tara was visiting Cripple Creek with her friend, Shelly, and they were staying at Dolly's. They were sitting at the bar having a drink when Kent came in. He sat next to Tara. Ed was bartending that night and introduced Kent to Tara and Shelly. Kent gave them a business card for Ms. Hattie's Bed & Breakfast and suggested they stay there the next time they came. On the next visit, Tara went by herself and stayed at Ms. Hattie's." She paused. "Is there something significant about this?"

"Only in the sense that it made me realize Tiffany must have been seeing someone in Cripple Creek. It didn't add up that she would come up here on the very weekend she was to show property to Jason Goldbloom. If she was seeing someone in Colorado Springs, I don't believe she would have come up that weekend. She hadn't been with the real estate company very long. As far as she knew, he was an important client who wanted to see some expensive property."

"Wait a minute, Joe, I'm getting confused. Didn't you tell me Jason Goldbloom lived in another state and he wasn't even here on that weekend?"

"That's right. He was in a hospital in St. Louis having surgery at the time of the murder. When I checked him out and personally talked to him, I concluded there is no way he made that appointment. The only time he'd ever been to Cripple Creek was the year before Tiffany died. He never even heard of her."

"So you're thinking someone deliberately set Tiffany up by using his name and credentials, which means someone planned Tiffany's death...but why?"

"That's the $64,000 question. When I figure *that* out, then I'll know who killed her."

"Even if she was seeing someone in Cripple Creek—and say he was the one who killed her—he had to have been planning her murder for a very long time. You don't come up with an elaborate scheme like that overnight. If he was just a visitor, as she was, it doesn't seem likely he would have had the time or resources."

"I know, and now I'm back to square one. For so long, my focus was in Colorado Springs, but I always came up short. I kept getting this hunch about Cripple Creek and finally switched my attention here. It's just a dumb ass hunch, but I can't let go of it. Every time I come up here I feel I'm going to latch onto something, but I always leave empty-handed. I wasted too much of my energy in Colorado Springs. And now, anyone here who might have seen Tiffany either doesn't remember her, or doesn't work here any longer. This brings me to the next item I want to discuss with you. In thinking about Tara coming to Cripple Creek to see Kent, I'm wondering if Tiffany could have been seeing someone locally. You mentioned reading Tara's diary. Does she say anything about meeting any of Kent's friends or any of the other locals from around here?"

"Gee, Joe, I don't think so. Other than mentioning Ed, Robert, and Al from Ms. Hattie's place, I haven't—as yet—read about anyone else she might have met."

Joe got up and started to pace. Both hands clasped behind his back, he stared at the ceiling and paced back and forth. Then he stopped abruptly and raised the question. "So you haven't finished the diary. There's still a chance she may have met some of Kent's friends or some of the locals."

"If you want the names of some men who might have met Tiffany or dated her, why don't you ask Kent yourself? Or Ed, for that matter—he probably knows most of the locals."

"Kelly, I'm not sure who I can trust. This is a small town. If somebody knows something, and they get suspicious of my questioning them, that news will spread like wildfire. Then folks may become uneasy and clam up."

"I see your point. Joe, I've wanted to finish Tara's diary while I'm here in Cripple Creek. This place, and everything she has experienced here, is what she writes the most about. After talking to Stan, I was anxious to get back home, but I can't see Max until next week. One more day won't matter. I'll stay and finish the diary. If I come across anything I feel might be helpful to your cause, I'll let you know."

"I would appreciate that, Kelly. I would appreciate it a lot."

"Well, Mr. PI, I'd better be getting back to my room. It seems I have a lot of reading to do."

Chapter Thirty-One

Kelly already had the key in her hand when she approached the door to her room. As she went to put the key in the lock, an ominous feeling came over her. She shrugged it off and unlocked the door. Once inside, she went straight to her suitcase to retrieve the diary. She didn't understand why, but she still continued to bury the diary in her suitcase under her nightgown—and she still kept her clothes in the suitcase rather than use the dresser. She reached under the nightgown to where she had placed the diary. Her first attempt proved unsuccessful. "Oh, come on, I know you're in here," she muttered. She moved her hand all around under the nightgown and even over to the other side, but she couldn't locate it. She panicked and threw the clothes to the floor. The diary wasn't there. She rummaged through the clothing, shaking out each piece individually as if the diary could have been stuck inside one of the garments.

"Oh, my God! Oh, my God!" she repeated. "Where is it!" She looked around the room and hoped she had laid it elsewhere, but she hadn't. *This doesn't make sense! The room looks normal. My clothes were still packed just the way I had left them. It doesn't look like anything has been touched. Then where's the diary?* She went through everything, over and over again. She pulled back the bedcovers and looked under the pillows. She even looked under the bed. Tara's diary was gone.

Kelly grabbed her phone to call Joe, but then stopped. *What if Joe had something to do with this? What if he lured me to his room so he could have someone break into my room and steal Tara's diary?* Then she paused, *Kelly! Get a grip!* She realized she was being paranoid. She knew Joe would not have confided in her if he had planned to steal Tara's diary. She called his cell from hers. She didn't want to use the room phone and have someone listen in on their conversation.

Joe answered on the first ring. He teased, asking if she needed more brandy to keep her comfortable while she read.

Kelly tried to relax. She didn't want to sound too frantic. After she told him what happened, he said he'd be right there. She asked if she should call the police.

"No. If there's no sign of a forced entry, and nothing else looks like it has been touched, the police will say you must have misplaced it or left it elsewhere. Whoever did this made sure to take great pains in leaving everything just as it was so it wouldn't look like anyone could have taken it."

"I did *not* misplace Tara's diary, nor did I leave it somewhere!" she said with a raised voice.

"I know, Kelly. You don't have to sell me. Listen, I'm on my way. Leave your door cracked so I don't have to knock. No need to alert anyone to my presence."

She hung up the phone and quickly straightened up the mess she had made.

When he arrived, Kelly again explained to Joe that she hadn't noticed anything being touched. And the clothes in her suitcase were exactly as she had left them… at least to the best of her recollection.

"I'm telling you, Joe, it just doesn't make any sense."

"Other than me, who knew you had the diary with you?"

"No one."

"Are you sure?"

"Maybe I should have said no one that I know of. But remember the episode I told you about at Ms. Hattie's? On the night I was sick and left my door open, I felt that someone had come in and picked up Tara's diary, because it wasn't the way I had left it."

"Yes, and I said in your ill state maybe you left it that way and just didn't remember."

"Well, what do you think now?"

"I think someone *was* in your room."

Kelly gave a sigh. "Joe, I just can't understand it. Why would someone want Tara's diary, and want it so badly that they'd go to all this trouble to steal it?"

"I don't know. You said the way you knew the diary had been touched the night you were sick was because it was put back facedown, something you would never do. Correct?"

"Yes, so…"

"Well, I hate to admit this, but at first I thought you were being a little paranoid about the facedown thing. I reasoned that, even if someone had picked up the diary, why turn it over when they put it back down? But then when I went back to my room, I picked up a book, started reading an interesting article, then marked it so I wouldn't lose my place and set it back facedown. So I've come to believe that your theory is plausible."

She didn't know whether to thank him for his vote of confidence or be annoyed that he thought she was paranoid. She felt he probably could tell what she was thinking by the look on her face. She wanted to say something, but decided to let it pass. After all, if he had told her such a story, she would have had questions about *him*.

Joe ignored the look and continued. "If someone picked the diary up, skimmed through to the back—especially if they were looking for something in particular—then it would make sense to hurriedly place it facedown. Kelly, I believe that someone was in your room at Ms. Hattie's and that they *did* look through the diary—and that's why the diary is missing now."

Kelly thought about what he said. "Joe, I agree with what you're saying, but I still don't understand. I haven't found anything in Tara's journaling that would have been of interest to anyone else. Unless..."

Joe broke in. "Unless that someone was Kent and he was curious to see if Tara had mentioned him. Is that what you're thinking?"

She didn't answer right away. She was thinking about the last entry she had read in Tara's diary. "No, that's not what I was thinking. I was actually thinking about Ms. Hattie, not Kent." She decided to tell him about Hattie's strange behavior after she discovered Tara and Kent had been together. The hurt Tara felt, and how confused she was by all of it. And after that weekend how Tara had to play down her feelings for Kent. She also told him how sad it was that Kent never knew how much Tara really cared about him.

"I don't know what to make of it all, Kelly, or what it may or may not have to do with the diary—but it does raise a lot of questions...which reminds me of something else I had wanted to ask you. Why did you decide to stay in Cripple Creek rather than leave once the roads were clear? Did it have anything to do with Tara's death?"

Kelly gave him a puzzled look. "No, of course it didn't. Tara died off a hiking trail at least 300 miles from here."

"Then why are you still here?"

"I can't really answer that...other than to say I felt the need to finish reading Tara's diary here. Maybe it's because she loved coming here—at least in the beginning." At that moment, she felt an unusual sensation, as if to validate that she should be there.

"I think it's more than that," Joe theorized. "In some strange way, your situation may be similar to my situation. Tiffany died in Colorado Springs, but I feel there's a connection to Cripple Creek."

It finally registered with Kelly what Joe was getting at. "Joe, you don't think someone in Cripple Creek might know what happened to Tara, do you?"

"Kelly, there are too many coincidences. I've got to try and sort it all out. I don't want to bog you down with all of it right now. You've had enough to deal with for one day. I'll get out of here and let you get some rest. Don't worry about the diary, we'll find it. I think we might be onto something. Let's meet later for dinner."

Kelly nodded and walked him to the door. She felt overwhelmed and was grateful for the time alone. She wanted to mentally process everything that had transpired. She lay across the bed and stared at the ceiling. *Why would anyone want Tara's diary?* she wondered. To her knowledge, the only people in Cripple Creek who knew Tara were Kent, Ms. Hattie, Robert, Al, and possibly Ed—but she wasn't sure if he'd remember her. And even if Kent knew about the diary, she couldn't imagine that he would have taken it.

She was deep in thought when the phone on the nightstand rang. She figured it had to be Joe but thought it strange that he didn't call her on the cell. Then it occurred to her it might not be him.

"Hello?" Kelly answered. The voice on the other end was muffled. She could hardly understand what they were saying. "I'm sorry, but I can't hear you, we must have a bad connection. Would you please call back?"

"Don't hang up," the caller said, "I have something of yours."

The voice was deep, distorted, and shaky. It reminded Kelly of someone on the news being interviewed who didn't want to be recognized. The station would conceal their face and alter the voice to protect their identity. She wasn't sure, but she thought she understood what was being said.

"Did you say you had something of mine?"

"Yes."

Kelly's heart began to race. She knew the person on the other end had to be talking about the diary, but she played ignorant. "Who is this? And what do you have of mine?" She hoped if she kept the conversation going, she might recognize who it was.

"I think you know what I have. I'm sure by now you've discovered that it's gone."

"If you have something of mine, you must want to return it, or you wouldn't be calling. Please speak louder and clearer—I'm having trouble understanding you. What was it you said you had?"

"I didn't say, but I know you know what it is. I'm not stupid, and neither are you. Listen, I don't want the diary—I just happened upon it. Meet me at the overlook on the outskirts of town and I'll give it back to you."

"Why don't you bring it here? And if you're so innocent, why disguise your voice?"

"I can't bring it there. I don't want anyone to see me, and if someone should be listening in, I don't want them to know who I am. I need to explain something to you. I know what really happened to Tara."

Kelly felt cold. She couldn't believe what she had heard, and for a moment, she felt like she was going to faint. She took deep breaths and told herself that in no way could she pass out—she had to meet this person. "I'm not sure I know where the overlook is."

"It's a couple of miles from town on the main road. You had to have passed it coming into Cripple Creek. It's a pull off on the right-hand side. They just cleared it of snow today. I have one more thing to say, and it is *very* important. You must come alone or our lives could be in jeopardy." The line went dead before Kelly had a chance to respond.

Without thinking, she called Joe, but he didn't answer. When his voice mail came on, she left him a message. She thought about what the caller said, *Come alone or our lives could be in jeopardy.*

Kelly wasn't concerned about meeting the stranger. She had frequently met people alone as an investigative reporter, and she had no qualms about doing it this time. She grabbed her purse and left.

Chapter Thirty-Two

J oe opened the door, threw his phone on the bed, and emptied his pockets. He decided to take a shower and change clothes. He knew once he started going through Tiffany's file, and tried to connect the dots, he'd be preoccupied. He wanted to look fresh for Kelly when they met for dinner.

Kelly had called while he was in the shower; he never heard the phone ring. It intermittently beeped to signify that he had received a call, but he was oblivious to it. He was focused on writing down notes while they were still fresh in his mind.

He went over everything he and Kelly had discussed and felt he was getting close to something big, but it just wouldn't come to him. Then he had a crazy idea. *Maybe Tiffany's and Tara's deaths were linked. Could it be possible that Tiffany and Tara came in contact with the same people? Could Tiffany have been seeing Kent five years before he met Tara? But even if she had been seeing Kent, it wouldn't explain her death or Tara's. Kent certainly had nothing to gain by anything happening to either one of them.*

Joe felt frustrated. He kept tapping the pad with his pen. *What am I missing? And what is that sound?* He finally realized it was his phone. When he saw he had a message from Kelly, he wasted no time in listening to it. All she said was she'd had a call about the diary, had to leave, and would catch up with him later. Joe quickly called her cell. There was no answer.

Chapter Thirty-Three

Her cell kept ringing, but she ignored it. She knew it had to be Joe. She was afraid that if she answered, he'd either try to talk her out of going or insist he meet her there. She wanted no part of either. The only way she could be sure to get the diary, and find out what happened to Tara, was to go alone.

Kelly had no trouble finding the overlook. It turned out to be a scenic turnoff that looked down on the entire town of Cripple Creek. It had been plowed—somewhat—but there still was a lot of snow. She drove into one of the vacant spaces. She didn't see another car, nor did she see any fresh car tracks. She put her cell phone in her coat pocket and got out of the car. She looked around to see if there was anyone else there—perhaps the caller had parked elsewhere—but she was all alone. She walked towards the front of the car and admired the view of the town below. She was cold and put her hands in her pockets.

Kelly had been in a situation like this only once before. She had been reporting on the suspicious disappearance of a wealthy businessman. An unidentified source called and asked to meet her in an abandoned building. He asked that she come alone, and she did. It was a worthwhile trip, and she had gained some valuable information that helped to prove the businessman had staged his own disappearance. He had been embezzling from his partner for years. The partner finally had the proof needed to press charges when the man disappeared. She thought about how she had felt when she waited in that abandoned building. She remembered feeling a little nervous and uneasy, but not frightened.

Five minutes passed and still no one showed. She decided to get back in her car, but just as she reached for the door, a car pulled up. She stood by the door and waited. The car pulled into the parking space at the opposite end of the overlook. It seemed like an eternity before someone finally got out. Kelly couldn't tell who it was. She felt her heart pound as the person walked towards her. She was confused. She had expected to be meeting a man; but the closer the stranger came, she could tell by the boots—even though they weren't the most feminine—and by the scarf around her face that it was a woman.

The approaching figure said nothing; she just continued to walk straight towards Kelly. When she got within four feet of her, she stopped.

"Did you come alone?" the woman asked. Her face was kept hidden by the scarf.

"Yes." Even though Kelly couldn't see the face, she caught a familiar tone in her voice. "You said you had the diary. Are you the one who took it? Where is it?"

"You'll find out soon enough. Right now I want to get out of here...I'm feeling a little conspicuous. See that tree over there?" She pointed to a large pine on the other side of a wooden railing. It was obvious the railing had been established to discourage visitors from venturing too far in pursuit of the perfect picture. "Let's go over there. I'll feel more comfortable."

"I'm not going anywhere until you tell me what you know about Tara's death."

"Don't be difficult, Kelly." She flashed a gun, and when she did, the scarf dropped from her face.

"I thought I recognized your voice, Carla. Why are you doing this? What do you want from me?" Kelly still had her hand in her pocket and felt for her phone. She found what she hoped was the send button. Joe was the last person she called. She knew if she pressed send, it would ring his cell. She'd have to talk fast and loud so he wouldn't hang up, but there was no guarantee he'd hear her.

"I'll tell you everything you want to know once we get over by the tree. I won't hurt you, Kelly, but I have to be sure I can trust you, and I don't want anyone passing by to see us."

Kelly didn't believe her. "Why did you want to meet here at this overlook?" she asked in a very loud voice. She kept throwing questions at her and called her by name, hoping Joe would catch some of it. "Wouldn't it have been better, Carla, to meet somewhere other than the overlook? Why do we have to go over by the tree? Why don't we sit in my car, Carla?"

"Shut up already, and quit yelling! I can hear you! I told you, we have to be careful not to be seen."

"Carla, if you don't intend to hurt me, why the gun?" She kept her voice loud.

"It tends to be more persuasive than I am, and I'm not sure that I can trust you. Besides, if I was going to kill you, don't you think I would have chosen a more secluded area?"

That did occur to Kelly, but it also occurred to her that she hadn't seen another motorist go by. It was the middle of the week, and even though the roads had been cleared—she felt most of the visitors wouldn't return until the weekend. If one of the residents drove by, they probably wouldn't pay any attention; but if they did, the gun was shielded by Carla's scarf.

"Keep walking, Kelly." Carla instructed.

They climbed over the wooden railing and gingerly maneuvered their way through the deep snow towards the tree—the warm sun the last couple of days did little to melt it. When Kelly looked in the area surrounding the tree, she noticed Mother Nature had swept the ground clear, forcing the snow into drifts elsewhere. As they approached it, it occurred to Kelly that if Carla was responsible for Tara's death, she wouldn't shoot her: if she was going to kill her, she would want it to look like an accident. Kelly suspected that Carla would threaten her with the gun and back her up until she stumbled and fell down the hilly terrain to her death. Or perhaps Carla would hit her over the head with a rock and push her to her death—just like what happened to Tara. Kelly reasoned that Carla would probably keep her alive until she was sure as to how much she knew, and what her connection to Joe was. She had to keep her talking. She knew if her call didn't go through to Joe, she was in serious danger.

"Okay, Carla. Tell me what this is all about," Kelly said loudly.

Carla had a smirk on her face. "Where should I begin? Should I begin with Tiffany Buckley?"

"Tiffany Buckley? Who's that?" I thought the reason I was here was to find out about Tara, and the diary! she shouted.

Kelly had to be careful of how much information she revealed. She wasn't sure what Carla was looking for, but she knew once she had it, keeping Kelly alive would no longer be important.

"Stop yelling, Kelly! You're making me nervous," she said and waved the gun at her. "It wouldn't be a good idea for me to be nervous while this gun is in my hand."

Kelly looked at the gun. She knew if Joe hadn't heard her by now, he never would, and she didn't want Carla anymore agitated than she already was. "Okay, Carla," she said in a normal tone, "what about this Tiffany Buckley?"

"I'm sure you know who she is—or was. I've seen how much time you've been spending with that cop. He *is* a cop, isn't he?"

"You mean Joe?"

"Yeah. Do you work for him?"

"Maybe I do and maybe I don't. Why should it matter to you whether I work for him or not? Do you think I'm onto something?" She wanted Carla to think she knew more than she did. And she wanted to draw her out and find out, if, and how, involved she was with Tiffany and Tara.

"If you work for him, then you probably know too much."

"Was it necessary for Tiffany to die?" Kelly asked the question as though she already had the answer. She looked around and spotted an old tree stump a foot from where they stood. She sat down and waited for the answer.

"Don't get too comfortable, Kelly. We're not going to be here that long. But I guess it doesn't matter now if I tell you everything. Actually, I think I'm going to enjoy watching the look on your face."

She began telling Kelly about the time she watched the front desk for Martha so Martha could go to the dentist. She went through the casino's records, looking for someone prosperous with a connection to Cripple Creek. She saw Jason Goldbloom's information and remembered waiting on him in the cafe. She knew he had built a golf course in Colorado Springs and lived elsewhere. She knew Tiffany was a real estate agent from Colorado Springs, so she put the two together and decided to use Mr. Goldbloom's information to set up the appointment.

"But it was a man who called pretending to be Mr. Goldbloom and set up the appointment with Tiffany. How did you pull that off?"

"That was the easy part. I had my buddy, Al, call and pretend he was Jason Goldbloom."

Kelly couldn't imagine Al having been involved in Tiffany's death. And she couldn't understand why Carla wanted Tiffany dead. "Did Al push Tiffany off the balcony?"

"Oh no, he wasn't even there. Besides, Al could never harm anyone. I just had him set up the appointment. I told him Mr. Goldbloom had asked me to make the appointment with Tiffany for him. I told Al I was running late for a doctor's appointment, then asked him if he would take care of it for me. Then, when it was time to meet for the showing, I called Tiffany and told her I was Jason Goldbloom's wife. I said we were running late and would meet her over at the house."

"Why would you want to kill Tiffany?"

"I didn't *want* to kill her. But there was no other way to keep her from seeing Kent. She was bad news. I would have been with Kent if it hadn't been for her. *I* was the one he really wanted until she poisoned him against me. He used to come in once every few weeks to visit his friend, Ed. He'd sit at the bar, have a drink, and chat with Ed about how busy, or slow, business was. If he was still there when I got off work, I'd sit at the bar and talk with him. I could tell he liked it when I sat down and talked to him. I knew he liked me more than he let on, but he was shy, and I know that's the only reason he didn't ask me out. That was okay with me, because I knew he'd ask me out one day. He was warm and friendly and made me feel like somebody."

Kelly listened nervously. Carla's mood fluctuated between rage when she talked about Tiffany to an eerie calmness when she spoke of Kent. One minute she was pointing the gun at Kelly, as though she were Tiffany, and the next minute she cradled it to her chest as if she was hugging Kent. It was clear to Kelly that any feelings Carla thought Kent might have had for her were strictly a fantasy built from her own desire.

Carla continued. "He came in to see Ed, but after a while, I think he just used that as an excuse. I know he really wanted to see me. I'm sure if he came in more often, he would have gotten up the nerve to ask me out. I dreamed about him day and night. It seemed like an eternity before he'd show up again. I couldn't stop thinking about him. But I know how shy people are, and I wasn't going to be pushy. Besides, as much as I thought about him, I knew he had to be thinking about me. And I felt the next time he came in would be the time he'd ask me out. But I didn't see him the next time he came in. He must have come in earlier and had to leave before I got off my shift.

"It was months before I saw Kent again. I had to work late one night, but when I left the cafe, I went by the bar. Kent was there, and sitting next to him was Tiffany. I didn't think too much about it at first and sat in the empty seat on the other side of him. He was friendly, but not his usual self. He seemed preoccupied. Then I noticed how Tiffany consumed his attention. I didn't blame Kent—he didn't stand a chance. I've seen her type before. She knew what she wanted and was determined to get it."

Carla raised her voice, and she began using her hands as she talked—aimlessly pointing the gun. Kelly watched her pace erratically and observed that a finger was kept on the trigger at all times. She knew it wouldn't take much for the gun to go off.

"What happened next, Carla?" Kelly asked in a calm voice, hoping to defuse her anger from escalating.

"After that first encounter, I could never catch Kent alone. He only seemed to come when she was there. She had some kind of hold over him. Then one night he came in and she wasn't there. I sat down and he bought me a drink. He was warm and friendly like he had been before. I could tell he had feelings for me, and if Tiffany hadn't come back, I know he would have asked me out. But five minutes later she appeared, and he acted as though I didn't exist. She had that much control over him.

"The next time she visited the casino, I told her to leave Kent alone. You know what she did? She told Kent. She must have made up lies and told him terrible things about me. She was that kind of person. I could tell she was evil. I know Kent cared for me, but Tiffany got in the way."

Kelly swallowed hard. She knew Carla was no one to reckon with. If she was going to get out of there alive, she had to stall Carla and keep her talking. But it was risky—Carla had become more agitated. "How do you know Tiffany told him what you said?"

"Kent showed up later that night after I had talked to Tiffany. They came into the cafe for coffee. She would look my way and whisper to him. When I came up to the table, Kent acted as though I wasn't even there. At first I thought it was because he didn't want her to know how he really felt about me until he could break away from her. But she did a number on him. I didn't go back to their table, but I could hear her laughing. I knew she was trying to poison him against me. But I showed her! Kent meant too much to me. I couldn't stand by and let her manipulate him into thinking I was no good for him. I could tell that's what she was doing."

Keep talking, Carla, keep talking. I have to keep you talking. "I can only imagine how surprised Tiffany was when you showed up instead of the Goldblooms."

Carla beamed as though she took great pleasure in remembering that moment. "It was great! I had already checked the house out and knew it had an upstairs balcony. That petite little bitch was no match for me."

Kelly continued quickly with more questions. She didn't want to give Carla time to think about what she would do to *her*.

"What did Kent do after Tiffany was out of the way?"

"He kept to himself for awhile. I guess she had more control over him than I realized. He had a hard time with her death and got more involved with the B & B, taking more of the responsibility away from Hattie. About two years ago he started coming into Dolly's again, at first to see Ed." Carla paused.

Kelly hurried with another question, one she really wanted an answer to. "How did you know about Tara's diary?"

"I was suspicious of you from the start. I watched you leave with Kent when he came to get you on the snowmobile. He didn't need another distraction in his life. I called Al and asked him to find out what he could about you. He said the first night you were there, Kent had hung your coat downstairs to dry. He went down about four in the morning and went through your pockets. He found nothing. He was going to check your door to see if you kept it unlocked so he could go in when he had the opportunity, but I guess you woke up and scared him off."

Kelly's head was swimming. She rapidly tried to put all the pieces together. It began to make sense...in a sick sort of way. But she still had questions. "Why would Al do that for you?"

"Are you kidding? I'm the only person who pays any attention to him. Hattie treats him like he doesn't exist most of the time. And he's always felt inferior to Robert. I told Al it was probably nothing, but I had concerns about you and would he do some checking for me. I made him feel important and needed. I treat him like he is somebody. The way Kent used to treat me. The way Kent started treating me again until Tara showed up."

"So Al must have been the one in my room the night I got sick at Ms. Hattie's."

"Yes. I had asked him to snoop through your things if he ever got the chance to get in your room. He told me about seeing the diary the night you were in the bathroom for so long. I got concerned Tara might have written in there about the time I called her and wanted to meet her on the Monument. You and Joe were spending too much time together. I was worried that when you compared notes, you'd put two and two together. So you see Kelly, I have no choice. Now get off that stump."

Kelly didn't move. She knew the end was near; Carla's behavior was very controlled, and she now had a determined calmness about her. The only chance she had was to keep her talking—and maybe somehow—take the gun away from her. "Why would Tara agree to meet you on the Monument?" she asked softly.

"She didn't," Carla continued, "at least not at first. I knew about the time Kent went hiking with her there. That's why I chose the place. I overheard Kent telling Ed that hiking the Monument was one of Tara's favorite things to do. So I called her and told her I'd be in the neighborhood and that I had a message and package for her from Kent. I said I had always wanted to see the Monument and asked if she would meet me there. She said she couldn't make it. That made me mad! I guess Miss Goody Two-shoes felt it was beneath her to accept something that wasn't hand delivered by Kent. Then I got a bright idea. I told her Kent didn't want me to tell her, but he was very ill...and that it would mean a lot to him if she would meet me. She finally agreed.

"Now, no more questions, Kelly. Get up." She waved the gun at her.

"Why, so you can hit me from behind with the gun and push me down the hill? I'm safe right where I am. I know you won't shoot me."

"Don't be so sure of yourself. Besides, I'm stronger than you, Kelly. I can knock you off of that stump. I have nothing to lose. You know everything."

"Except how you got into my room. Tell me, Carla, how did you accomplish that?"

"That was easy," Carla told her. "I distracted Martha long enough to steal the duplicate key. I saw you and Joe go back to his room. I figured you'd be there awhile. Kelly, if I have to shoot you, I will. My car is packed and I'm ready to leave town. By the time anyone figures this out—if they ever do—I'll be long gone. I've had enough of this town and the people in it. Maybe when I'm gone, Kent will realize how much he really does care for me."

Kelly stayed still. She was frightened beyond belief, but she wouldn't give Carla the satisfaction of letting her know it. Her phone must not have connected to Joe's. She wondered if he'd wait for her at dinner, not knowing she was dead.

A voice in Kelly's head started yelling. *Fight! Fight!* Out of nowhere came a burst of energy.

Carla was angry that she couldn't make Kelly get up. She went over and kicked her, then pushed her off the stump. She grabbed Carla's leg and they rolled and rolled. Carla punched her in the eye, and Kelly fell back and hit her head on a rock. She couldn't get up; she felt woozy and thought she was going to pass out. She heard

Carla fire the gun—not once, but twice. She felt nothing. She knew she must be dead. She was in and out of consciousness. She thought she heard Tara call her name. Then she heard her father call her name. Faintly at first, then it got louder.

"Kelly! Kelly! Are you alright?"

"Joe!" She slowly sat up with his help, her head still spinning. She touched her face, then her arms and legs. "I haven't been shot, but I heard the gun." She looked behind Joe and saw the police.

"Carla's dead, Kelly. They had to shoot twice. After the first shot, she pointed the gun at the officer. He fired again."

"Oh, God," Kelly felt sick. She didn't know if it was due to the bump on her head, or knowing that Carla was dead, or because she was almost killed. "Joe, you won't believe it! Tiffany! Tara! It was Carla."

"I gathered that by what I could hear of the conversation."

"My cell went through?"

"How else did you think I found you? Nice piece of detective work, Ms. Kelly Murphy. Maybe you should change careers. I could use someone like you in my office."

She put both hands on her throbbing head and moaned, "Work for someone as slow as you? I was almost killed! What took you so long?"

The officer looked at both of them. Joe winked at him.

"She's delusional, officer. I'd better get her out of here and see to it she gets the help she needs." He scooped Kelly up in his arms and carried her to his car.

"Put me down, Joe. I don't need to be carried."

"The hell you don't," he said with a smile. She looked up at him and smiled back.

Chapter Thirty-Four

Joe had planned to take Kelly to the hospital if the ambulance hadn't arrived, but before he got to his car, they showed up. Against her protest, she was taken to Pikes Peak Regional Hospital in Woodland Park, where they kept her overnight for observation. The doctor said that she was very lucky to have suffered no more than a mild concussion.

Before leaving Cripple Creek, Kelly went back to Ms. Hattie's Bed & Breakfast. There was some unfinished business she wanted to take care of. When Ms. Hattie opened the door, it was obvious she wasn't pleased to see her. Kelly said she needed to talk with her, but that she'd like for Kent to join them. Hattie hesitated a moment, then invited her in. There was something in Kelly's tone of voice that caused her not to question. She left Kelly in the parlor and went looking for Kent.

Kelly walked over to the wood-burning stove and took a deep breath. She smelled the hardwood and thought about her father, remembering how he could always make the perfect fire. She reflected on the years past: her failed marriage to Mark; her father's Alzheimer's; her mother dying and never forgiving her for putting her in a nursing home; and Tara, her best friend, murdered. If she had gone hiking with Tara that day, would she have died, too? Or would Tara still be alive? Her thoughts vanished when Kent and Ms. Hattie entered the room.

"Hello, Kelly," said Kent. "It's nice to see you again. Mother said there was something you wanted to discuss with us."

"Yes, Kent, there is. I'm sure you'll be hearing about it soon enough, but I wanted you both to hear it from me first."

"Please be seated, Kelly," said Ms. Hattie.

Kelly sat on the sofa, leaving the two high-back chairs for Kent and Hattie. Kent was focused. Hattie seemed anxious and fidgeted with her hands.

Kelly began. She filled them in with everything that had happened since she left the B & B, starting with Tara's diary being stolen. Kent let out a gasp when it registered that, unbeknownst to him, having been friendly with Carla is what cost Tara her life. Hattie just kept repeating, "How could I have been so blind?" When Kelly finally finished, the room was totally still, as though the air had been sucked right out of it. The quiet was deafening. There was more Kelly wanted to say, but she gave them a moment with their thoughts. Then she looked straight at Kent and broke the silence.

"Kent, there's something I know Tara would have wanted me to tell you. After reading her diary, it was obvious to me that she cared tremendously for you."

"Then why, Kelly—*why* did she refuse to see me anymore?" Kent said with tears in his eyes. Hattie held tight to her clutched hands: not knowing whether Tara wrote about her last visit to the bed-and-breakfast, she gave a pleading look to Kelly. Kelly would have liked to have told Kent about how awful his mother had been to Tara, and that's why Tara quit seeing him; but Hattie looked so fragile, so broken, that she couldn't get herself to do it.

"Kent, Tara had a lot going on in her life at that particular time. Maybe once she sorted out some things, she would have gotten back in touch with you—but maybe not. I can't say for sure. And possibly the distance was a factor. I do know that Tara would want you to get on with your life. Tara would want you to be happy," she said as she glanced at Hattie. She continued to fill them in on everything else that Carla had done. She told them about Tiffany Buckley, and about how Carla had used Al to help her. "Al may have helped Carla, but he had no idea what she was up to, and I don't think the police will even question him."

Kent and Hattie were speechless, and tried to absorb all that Kelly had said; and then they looked at her and told her that they were glad she was alright— and glad that Carla would never be able to hurt anyone else again. Kelly thanked them, then got up to leave. Hattie took her hand, and whispered in her ear, "Kelly, I am genuinely sorry that I misjudged Tara. I hope one day you'll find it in your heart to forgive me." Kelly nodded, but deep down she didn't know if that day would ever come.

Kent walked Kelly to the door. He thanked her for letting them know what had happened to Tara. Hattie stood by the window in the parlor. As she looked towards the hall, she saw Robert's shadow. She suspected he had overheard the conversation. She walked into the hallway and, seeing him, stopped. He looked at her with the utmost compassion. Her eyes filled, and without saying a word, she went to him. He opened his arms, and she welcomed his embrace.

Epilogue

J oe went back to Colorado Springs and Kelly returned to the Western Slope. Tara's diary, found in Carla's car, was returned to Kelly. She visited Tara's grave, taking the diary with her, and finished reading it while she was there: it seemed appropriate. The next thing she did was—according to Stan—write one of her best articles. She told about what had really happened to Tara; but more than that, she honored the life Tara had lived and the special friendship they shared.

Four weeks had passed since that fateful night with Carla. Tara's murder had been solved, but Kelly hadn't felt the closure she expected. She thought she was grieving even more now than she had when Tara died. She felt sad and lonely and missed Tara desperately. Stan felt Kelly had gone back to work too soon. He told her to take a long weekend and rest up. Kelly protested, but she knew she was in a state of inertia and that she was struggling to be productive. Every emotion she had suppressed for the last few years had surfaced. Not only was she consumed with the grief of having lost her childhood friend, but she experienced all over again the losses of her father and mother. She wondered if she had done everything possible for them while they were alive. Was she the daughter she should have been? Could she have been a better friend to Tara?

It was a Saturday night. She had been home all day, with very little to do, and no work assignments to keep her busy. She had too much time on her hands, and the emptiness felt huge. She went to bed early.

Kelly had been in a deep sleep when she awakened for no apparent reason. She sat straight up in bed and felt surrounded by a warm, comforting feeling. The night lamp in the living room was still on—it was clearly visible from her bedroom. She knew it wasn't midnight yet, as that was when the lamp was programmed to shut off.

She felt compelled to look past the lamp towards the counter entering the kitchen. She felt the goose bumps, and then saw the figures. First her father, and then her mother. They held hands and smiled. Soon, another figure joined them. It was Tara. A soft light surrounded her, and she looked happy. Kelly closed her eyes and shook her head. She thought she must have been dreaming. When she opened her eyes, they were still there. This time they had their arms around each other and smiled peacefully. Then their images began to fade. Kelly tried to speak—she didn't want them to leave—but nothing came out. Then just as quickly as they had appeared, they were gone. The goose bumps left and she felt a calmness she had never experienced before. As if instructed, she lay back down and became very tired. Just before she succumbed to sleep, she heard a soft voice whisper: *You were a wonderful daughter, and the best of all friends. You must let go and live your life.*

The next morning she wakened to the ringing of her phone. She knew it was probably Joe. He had left a couple of messages before, but she couldn't get herself to call him back. Now she felt different. She jumped out of bed and grabbed the phone. There was no sorrow or grief weighing her down. She was at peace.

"Hello?"

"Hi, Kelly, it's Joe. I can't believe you answered… this must be my lucky day."

"Sorry about not getting back to you. You can't imagine how hectic it's been. I'm still playing catch-up." It was easier to let him think she was too busy than try to explain her state of grief.

"I read your article about Tara. It was great, Kelly. That's one of the reasons I'm calling."

"Thanks, Joe. How did it go for you when you told Tiffany's parents how she really died?"

"It was tough, but at least it brought the closure they needed. And thanks to you, I was able to keep my promise to them and find the person responsible. Kelly, the other reason for calling—and I know this is short notice—but I'll be over on the Western Slope later this afternoon and I was hoping you would have dinner with me."

"What brings you over here?"

"That's a good sign! You didn't say 'no' right away! Actually, I'm working on a case and I'm following up on a lead. I'll be within thirty miles of you. I figure it's worth driving the extra thirty to pick your brain for awhile." He knew that would get her attention.

"I should have known it was my mind you were after."

"Well, I have to start somewhere. I take it that's a yes?"

She paused, but for only a second. "Yes, I guess so. But I want you to know it will be a sacrifice, having to give up watching my reruns. Tell me where and what time. I'll meet you there. You won't have any trouble recognizing me. I'll be the one wearing the brain." She heard Joe laugh. It felt good to hear his laughter.

"And to think, I thought you'd be glad to see me," he said, chuckling as he continued. "I can't risk the chance you might forget to wear your brain. I'll come pick you up. Give me your address. I should be there by seven." They joked a little more, then Kelly gave him directions to her house.

"If I'm running late, I'll give you a call."

"Sounds good. I'll see you around seven."

"Kelly, I'm really looking forward to seeing you."

"Me too, Joe."

She hung up the phone and walked to the window. The sun was out, and the sky was blue. She thought about her father, mother, Tara, and the visit she'd had from them. She knew they wouldn't need to come back again. She understood the message: she was ready to move on. A bird landed on the still-bare limb of the aspen tree and chirped. It was a little early for spring, but Kelly knew that a new season had begun for her.